KEEP HIM WILD

KELLY MOORE

Edited by KERRY GENOVA

Illustrated by DARK WATER COVERS

Photography by PAUL HENRY SERRES

Kelly Moore

KEEP HIM WILD

Keep Him
WILD

WHISKEY RIVER WEST

KELLY MOORE

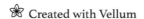 Created with Vellum

BLAISE

"You haven't graced me with your charming presence in a couple of weeks. How are you?" She rocks her pen back and forth between her long, slender fingers.

"Good to middling. Actually, fantastic." I stride to her desk. "I brought you coffee." Twisting the to-go cup from the tray, I hand it to her.

"Sounds like a man in complete denial to me," she retorts as a small frown burrows between her eyebrows. "You know what coffee I drink?"

"Caramel latte with an extra shot." I grin as I perch on her leather couch.

"Ah, from your player toolbox." She removes the lid and sets it to the side.

"My what?" I laugh.

"You're admittedly a player, and it's one of your resources you use to pick up women. Knowing what they like gives you the upper hand."

I shrug a single shoulder. "I pay attention, that's all."

She stands, straightens her pencil skirt, and then picks up her laptop, swaying her hips to the over-sized comfy chair in front of me. She sits, crossing her legs.

"What would you like to talk about today?"

"Nothing really. I just missed your beautiful face." She's professional and has mastered the art of not letting her eyes roll, enduring my sarcasm. *Evie Shields, Licensed Therapist.* My thoughts scatter to the first time I set foot in her office not long after moving to Missoula. I didn't care for her at first because she saw right through my facade. It's hard when you can't hide from someone. My flirting had no effect on her hazel eyes. She's a good ten years older than my thirty years and not my type. She's too professional for my liking. I'm more into the natural, down-to-earth type of gal who's not afraid to get her hair messy or show off her freckles. Even her office speaks volumes about her with black-and-white city prints and a stark modern look, but she is very attractive, and she's got some damn fine long, sexy legs. Legs that would...

"Eyes up here," she says, calling me out. "Are you still taking your medication?"

"It's hit and miss most days."

"We've talked about this before. You need to take it daily without fail for it to work properly. Are you sleeping?"

"That's hit or miss too." I sit back on the couch, bracing my arm on the back of it, and sit with an ankle propped on my knee.

"Talk to me, Blaise." She shuts her laptop and focuses solely on my face.

"I thought today would be a flyover sort of day." A nondescript sound escapes my lips, and my jaw hardens.

"You've gotten way too good at analyzing the hell out of anything that makes you uncomfortable so you can box it up, put a label on it, and stuff it in your closet, metaphorically speaking," she adds. "What made today not a flyover day?" She throws my own words back at me.

"Most of the time, I feel like I'm watching a movie and going through it line by line. When I try to step into the character I'm playing from memory, I melt. Like my heart drips from being frozen if that makes any sense." The Italian leather squeaks as I squirm on the cushion.

"It makes complete sense to me."

I sit in silence, not wanting to spill my guts.

"A long time has passed since the incident occurred. In fact"—she pops open her laptop then shuts it— "today is an anniversary of sorts. Have you ever tried being in a serious relationship?"

"No." I swallow hard and say her name. "When Rachel committed suicide twelve years ago, I swore to myself I'd never have that type of connection with anyone again because I couldn't bear the crippling fear of a surprise ending."

"So you go into every relationship with an expiration date at the beginning?"

I plant my feet on the ground. "Not a specific date, but I knew, yes. I felt safe in knowing that it would end because I planned it that way. In my head, I checked boxes as to the timing of it."

"You closed off your heart so when the end came, you could justify it."

"Exactly. No tears. No melodramatic loss." My gaze falls to the floor. Admitting I'm an ass when it comes to women is a hard nut to swallow.

She flips open her computer, and I lift my eyes to see what she's doing. She reads from her notes. "The last time you were in my office, we discussed your emotional detachment when you kiss a woman. Has that changed?"

"You mean a kiss feeling mechanical, no pleasure stemming from it?"

She peers over the top of her computer. "You've got a good memory. That was almost verbatim."

"It's hard to forget when that's how it feels," I mumble, closing my eyes.

"Do you show this vulnerable side to anyone but me?"

"I'm not vulnerable," I protest, not wanting to own it and squaring my shoulders.

"Being unguarded isn't a negative quality, Blaise. It's how you start making a connection, letting people into your life to see the real you."

"I may have a pretty face, but the real me is ugly on the inside." My thumbs fight with one another, spinning in my lap.

She snickers. "You don't need an ego boost, that's for sure."

"I'm tired of being alone and my relationships being meaningless, but I don't know how to change what I feel on the inside. After all these years, I still wake up in the middle of the night drenched in sweat, drowning in my nightmares. But every now and then, I dream I'm being suspended over a cliff, weightless and safe because whoever's face is blurred in my dreams is holding me, not letting me fall, and in those moments, it feels damn good."

"That's progress trying to happen within you. I have a task for you"— she holds out her hand to keep me from responding—"not that you'll come back, you tell me that every time, but I want you to take a risk with a woman, not someone from your harem of girls you've dated. I want you to lean into that feeling of being held weightless over a cliff and be open to trusting that you won't be dropped. Step outside of that script in your movie and allow the opportunity for a leading lady to know you without having previously read the lines."

"You make it sound so simple." I chuckle. "Who truly wants a man that battles with depression every day?"

"I've seen you out and about in town. You hide it very well."

"That's what I'm afraid of. What happens when I fall, and it doesn't stay hidden?"

"The medication I prescribed will help you with that."

"I just want to feel normal and not depend on meds."

"Who's to say what normal feels like?" She angles over her computer, clasping her hands at her knees. "We've had enough sessions that I think I can speak frankly to the man inside of you. He's smart and has a humongous heart. A man whose family adores him and is great with kids. You have so much to offer, and yet you hold yourself back and let everyone else in your life believe that you're alright."

"You left out handsome, strong, and very skilled with my hands," I chide with a smirk and a waggle of my eyebrows.

She bursts out laughing. "Yes, those things too, but that's outwardly. I'm talking to the man living inside that heart of yours."

I get to my feet. "You mean the heart that's frozen."

She gets up and moves beside me. "So let someone thaw it out. I think you're ready. Besides, if you don't try, I've failed at my job, and failure has never been an option for me."

"It's obvious from all the diplomas on your wall." I hike a finger over my shoulder at the one anchored above the couch.

"This isn't about me. Even your dreams are telling you it's time to let go and give love another chance. Do you recall how it felt to be in love at eighteen years old?"

"What's vivid in my mind is the pain. It detached me from feeling anything."

"That's not true. You love your family and would die for them. You've told me that several times in our sessions."

"That's because I know no matter what, they won't let me falter off of the cliff no more than I would them. Do you think I like screwing women and feeling absolutely nothing for them? I know it makes me a prick in the worst way."

"Have you ever promised any of these women more than a roll in the hay?" Her brow raises.

"No."

"Then they've allowed it. The blame game isn't one-sided."

"I think I've been shrink-juked by you enough today." I chuckle and take the few steps to her office door.

"At least contemplate what we've discussed and give yourself a chance to truly be happy. Maybe you won't need the medication, but in the meantime, keep it consistent." She holds the door open. "I'll see you in a week."

"Don't count on it." I half laugh, sprinting out to meet Walker at the brewery for dinner.

As soon as I walk in the door, one of the waitresses I've hooked up with on occasion saunters my way.

"Hey, cowboy," she purrs, eye-fucking me up and down. Her hand slips to the back of my neck, pulling me close to whisper in my ear. "I can take five if you want to join me in the ladies' bathroom."

I rarely let a proposition of sex go by from a willing partner, but the conversation with my therapist tumbles around in my head for a bit. Planting my hands in the pockets of my jeans, I take a step back. "I'm meeting my cousin for dinner."

Her disappointment is obvious when she mashes her bright red lips together."You know where I am if you change your mind."

I won't. I will. No, I won't, I war in my head. "I see my cousin," I say, scooting by her before my cock, who's been my partner in crime, overrides me.

"You're late," Walker grumbles. "I took the liberty of ordering you a beer." He taps the brown bottle on the counter, and I take the barstool next to him.

"Sorry. I had a meeting I had to make."

"Meeting as in your therapist?"

"How'd you—"

"Jace called me last night and asked me to keep an eye on you. It's the anniversary of Rachel's death."

"Another cousin who needs to mind his own damn business," I huff, taking a swig of my beer.

"Cut him some slack. He's just worried about you, man. You two used to be thick as thieves growing up."

"I'm sure we will be again when he moves here in a few weeks."

"Jace is coming to Montana? How did I miss that?"

I squint. "Probably because you've been a little preoccupied with Kat. You'll officially be a married man after this weekend." I clasp his shoulder.

"It will be the best day of my life. I never thought it would happen."

"I'm happy for you."

"I wish you'd settle down and give up your wild ways."

"You and my mother." I laugh. "And apparently, my therapist."

"There's got to be some woman in this town you'd be willing to settle down for."

"I haven't met one yet." I release a frustrated sigh and take the last pull from my beer bottle.

The microphone buzzes and a man taps it, announcing the start of karaoke hour. Two young women bebop onto the stage. One of which I've seen before; the other must be new in town. As soon as they start to sing, the brunette mesmerizes me with her voice, deep down, disturbingly so. She twists a lock of her hair between her fingers as she belts out the words. With the other hand, she grips the microphone, and it makes me wish it was my cock she was holding so firmly.

"Damn, she's good. What the heck is she doing singing in a no-name place like this? She belongs in Nashville." Walker spins on his barstool to face the stage.

"Yeah, but then I wouldn't get the chance at the possibility of tumbling in the hay with her if she were in Nashville singing." I nudge him in the ribs with my elbow.

"That young woman is too good for the likes of your sorry ass. You don't have to bed every female in town." He aims his beer bottle at her.

"What would be the fun in that?" I grin.

"I challenge you to get to know her and not sleep with her. And by sleeping, I mean not screwing her brains out," he dares me.

I gnaw the inside of my cheek, envisioning all the ways I could use her lips, and then blink them away. "I'll take your challenge." *Why? Because I know I'll fail, and I'll still get laid.*

2

THAYER

"I'm still in shock that you actually moved to Montana. Big city girl arrives in the country." Sage, who's been my best friend since I was fifteen, gestures around the room as we sit cross-legged in the middle of her living room floor, sipping on wine.

"I have to admit, it feels a bit surreal to me. Don't get me wrong, what you've shown me this last week is beautiful and so much more peaceful than the city."

"You're going to love it here once you get over the culture shock. I was never a fan of Boston, but I didn't have a say in whether my father was stationed in Fort Devens. The one good thing it brought me was you. Your friendship through high school is what kept me sane."

"College would've been more fun if you would've hung around."

"Boston College was not my scene. My love is for photography and nature. Yours was literature."

"Didn't you say you're working a photo shoot for a wedding this weekend? I wouldn't call that nature." I chuckle.

"My wedding and party gigs pay the bills. The other is what I love, and one day I'll have a gallery in town to display all my works of art."

"And I'll be here to support you." I hold her hand. "Thank you for letting me run away to your house."

"There's no place I'd rather you be. Being that you're three thousand miles away from your stalker makes me feel better too."

"Yeah, I'm glad that's over. Whoever thought a novelist would have a stalker?" I reach past her to the coffee table and pour another glass of wine.

"You are knockout gorgeous"—she flips a strand of hair over my shoulder—"and very talented." She polishes off her glass of wine, and I refill it. "Speaking of talent, the local brewery has karaoke in about an hour. Do you want to go?"

"I look a mess, and I don't feel like getting all made up."

"That's what's great about this place. You don't have to. The people here are different. Natural beauty is a real thing. I don't recall the last time I painted on makeup."

I bite the corner of my lip. "It would be fun to get out."

She puts her glass down and takes mine, setting it on the table, then hops to her feet, dragging me with her. "You might meet some hot cowboy."

"I've never been into cowboys," I snicker.

"That's because you've never experienced their raw sexiness," she coos.

"Oh, do tell," I snort, following her into her closet.

"The best sex I've ever had." She giggles.

"Where is this handsome cowboy of yours?"

"I dumped him like a hot potato when I found out he was engaged."

"No," I gasp.

"Yeah. I'll do my research next time before I jump in bed with a man. You should totally wear this." She holds out a soft white cotton dress with spaghetti straps.

"I don't know." I frown. "Looks a little simple to me."

She snags my hand and tosses the dress on the bed. "None of your city clothes will work here." She grabs the hem of my blouse, tugging it over my head. "You'll look hot in this."

"Fine," I cave, kicking out of my slacks.

"Take those off too." She gestures to my bra and panties.

"What?"

"You heard me."

"I'm not stepping foot outside these four walls without undergarments." I'm sure my eyes are wide as I stare at her in disbelief.

"Come on. Don't be such a prude. It's a freeing feeling."

I blow out a long breath. "You win," I say, wiggling out of my panties, unsnapping my bra, and pulling the dress over my head. "Feels weird." I run my hands down my hips, flattening the dress.

"You look beautiful, and you'll have a cowboy eating out of your hand in no time." She ushers me into the bathroom and shoves a brush at me.

"With no panties on, they'll be wanting to eat something, but it won't be my hand." I snatch the brush from her, and she bursts into a full-on smile.

"That's the spirit."

Turning toward the mirror, I brush out my long brunette hair and tuck it behind my ears. "I'm not looking for a one-night stand or a relationship. You see how the last one turned out."

She rummages through a drawer and holds out a tube of lip gloss. "This is my new favorite."

"I should really put at least a splash of makeup on." I lean into the mirror and rub my hands over my cheekbones.

"You don't need it." She spins me around, and before I can protest, she's dabbing my lips.

"It takes like mango." I rub my lips together.

"Look in the mirror."

I have to admit, I do like the simpler look, and I feel like the girl inside me rather than the one that always has to be on for other people. "I like it," I whisper.

She disappears and returns in a flash, tossing on a pink flannel shirt and a pair of jeans.

"How come I'm in a dress and you're in pants?"

"Because that look suits you way better than me. You'll need this." She flings a jacket at me.

"Denim," I scowl.

"Trust me when I tell you that denim will be your new best friend around these parts. Just wait until you see a sexy cowboy strutting in a pair of Wranglers. There ain't nothing like it."

Shrugging on the jacket, I face the mirror. "I'll have to take your word on it."

"I just so happen to have an extra pair of cowgirl boots." She pulls one on her foot and then points to a pair of black ones in the corner.

"This will be a first." I lean down to get them.

"I'm going to make you a country girl yet," she beams.

"I've missed you. You always try to get the real me to shine."

She hops to her feet and ties her hair in a knot. "Let's go. I want us to be the first ones on stage."

"You are way too excited about this. Are you sure there's not some studly cowboy your aching to hook up with? Because if that's the case, I could stay here and work on my manuscript."

"Not a chance I'm leaving you home tonight. I'm only excited that we get to go out and have some fun. Just us girls." She links her arm with mine once she's locked the door.

The spring air has a coolness in it that has me drawing the denim jacket over my breasts. Good thing because my nipples are poking through the white cotton material. It's a short drive from the outskirts of town to Main Street. We lucked out and found a place to park underneath a street light.

"This place is great. It's a brewery serving food and drinks, but it has a dance floor and a stage. You're going to love the atmosphere." She strolls in as if she owns the place, speaking to several people on the way to the hostess stand. The guy behind the stand grins and hugs her, and takes us to a table right away despite the line outside.

"I take it he's a friend of yours," I shout so she can hear me over the music playing on the speakers.

"He's my brother's best friend from the military."

"That explains it." I hold on to the strap of her purse, following her to the table right in front of the small stage.

"Thanks." She kisses him on the cheek, and he weaves his way back.

"Who knew a small-town bar would be standing room only." I drag my chair from underneath the table and sit.

"It's like this every karaoke night."

"There's no way we're going to be the first to sing."

"My name is always on the top of the list in case I show up."

"Should I ask who you slept with to make that happen?" I howl.

She makes a zipping motion over her mouth and then smiles.

Waving the waitress over, she orders two longneck beers. I take a minute to check out the crowd. Sage was right. Cowboys do look good in their blue jeans and silvery belt buckles. Most of the men appear to belong here, but there's one man sitting at the end of the bar that makes me think of the type of men I'd see back home. Dressed in a tailored suit with a knotted silk tie, hunched over the bar, motioning for a refill. A solo drinker, oblivious to the makeup-caked cougars aiming for his wallet. The women swarming him look like they want a way to escape a small town. Most all the other women in the bar are exactly as Sage said, natural in their own beauty.

Right as our beers show up, a man takes the mic and announces karaoke night. Sage snatches my hand, and we get up on the stage. She peers through the list of songs and points, wearing a cheesy grin. "Who doesn't love the Dixie Chicks?"

She introduced me to "Goodbye Earl" the first day we met. "I think this crowd will love it."

I belt out the words, and as we sing, I scan the bar. My gaze sets on a devilishly handsome man straddling a barstool with an amber bottle resting against his lips. My body tingles just looking at him. I briefly glance away, and when I look back, he's removed his cowboy hat, and his bright green eyes are dancing with my light browns. His cappuccino-colored hair is cut short on the sides, but the waves on top give him a messy look, and out of nowhere, my fingers itch to run through it. His smile is dazzling, with pretty white teeth. He stands, and every hard curve of his muscled body is apparent through his dark, tight, short-sleeved Henley with the three buttons undone. Thank the Lord I can't see his backside, or I'd stammer over the lyrics, making a complete fool of myself. It's bad enough I'm drooling over the gorgeous-as-hell stranger.

I break my enchantment with him when the song ends, and we high-five one another as the crowd of people in the brewery applauds us with claps and whistles.

We return to our table, and I gulp down my long-neck that's no longer chilled, but it stifles the burning in my gut.

"That was awesome!" Sage squeals, flagging down the waitress again. "We'll have two cheeseburgers and lots of fries," she tells her.

"You know I don't eat greasy food."

"You will tonight. Trust me, you're gonna love it. You've never had hamburgers that taste like this where you come from."

I can't stop my gaze from roaming to the stranger at the bar. Women are all over him, vying for his attention. The other cowboy sitting next to him smiles and waves at Sage.

"Who is that?"

"He's the groom in the wedding I'm shooting this weekend. If he weren't married, I'd be all over him." She waves back.

"Who's the cowboy sitting beside him?"

"The one with the girls fawning all over him?" She crinkles her nose.

"He is pretty fine-looking."

"I'd steer clear of him if I were you. Unless you're looking to wake up to an empty bed in the morning."

"Is this coming from the voice of experience?" I raise a quizzical brow.

"Believe me, he's very tempting, but he's nothing but a player, and I don't want anything to do with getting my heart broken."

"I don't know...I might risk being a glutton for punishment." I lick my lips, admiring his physique.

"Don't do it. There are dozens of other cowboys to choose from in this town."

I exhale and scoot my chair so that I can't gawk at him anymore. "You're right. I don't need trouble. I've already had enough of that for a lifetime."

She scrunches her cheek, closing one eye. "You do know you're only twenty-five, right? Trouble is bound to find you somewhere along the road, just not with the likes of him."

Our food is set in front of us, and it smells heavenly. One bite and the juices from the burger are running down my chin.I reach for a napkin and find a rugged hand with stained nails on top of it. My sight trails up his arm to an up close and personal look at the gorgeous cowboy.

"Something must be wrong with my eyes because I can't take them off of you." Even his voice is sexy. I wonder how many times he's used that pickup line.

The man next to him steps in. "I'm Walker. This is my not-so-subtle cousin, Blaise."

Damn, even his name sets me on fire.

"Are you ready for Saturday?" Sage comes to the rescue when I've apparently forgotten how to speak.

"I can't wait to marry my beautiful bride." Walker's smile is so genuine you can feel his love for her.

"I didn't catch your name?" The cowboy hands me my napkin.

"This is my best friend, Thayer. She moved here from Boston a week ago," Sage says without the smile she was wearing.

"We won't keep you ladies," Walker says with his hand on Blaise's shoulder. He ignores it and pulls out the chair next to me, spinning it around and straddling it. "I like your name. It's very unusual."

"Why don't you join us?" I mutter and take another bite of my hamburger.

"Thanks for the invite," he beams, stealing a French fry.

"She was being sarcastic." Sage folds her arms over her chest.

Blaise mashes his sexy lips together and stands. "It was a pleasure to meet you, Thayer. I hope you make yourself comfortable in our little town."

I nearly choke on my food when he turns around, and his sweet jeans hug his ass. "Oh, my god," I whisper wide-eyed to Sage. I wish I was blind at this moment because his bad boy alarm has me squeezing my thighs tight. He's the type of man I write about in my novels. The one that breaks

3

BLAISE

"Damn, did you see those eyes?" I glance over my shoulder.

"She wasn't interested," Walker squawks. "Plus, I'd like there to be no issues at my wedding, and being that she's my photographer's best friend, she's forbidden."

"What if she's the one?" I grit out, returning to our barstools.

"I highly doubt it, but if she is, you can postpone your cock fest until after I've tied the knot."

I rub my hands over my thighs. Her hair looked so soft that I wanted to run my fingers through it. And that dress she was wearing—my teeth ached to lean down and snag the straps between them to expose her pale skin. The smell of mango had my dick twitching. I've never wanted to lock lips with a woman so badly. A kiss has always been meaningless to me, but with her... I repeatedly blink, shaking the dirty thoughts from my head. "I'm going back over there." I go to stand, but Walker snags my forearm.

"Did you not hear me ask you to stay away from her until after the wedding? I'm sure Sage has told her by now that you're a horn dog. I'd just let it go."

He's right. Besides, there are plenty of women in this bar I could go home with and blow off some steam. But, for once, I'm not interested. I sit and chat with Walker while watching the gorgeous creature from the corner of my eye. What is it about her that has me so frazzled?

Her lips?

Her eyes?

Her taut nipples?

The way she belted out the words to the song?

Or simply her natural beauty?

Whatever it is, I'm going to find out, but it will have to wait until after the wedding.

I excuse myself to the restroom and have to fight off the waitress that hit on me the minute I walked in the door. Walker is waiting for me with my Stetson in his hand when I get back. I toss cash on the bar and file out the door behind him.

"What is it with you and women? Do you exude pheromones or what?" He chuckles. "There wasn't one woman in there that didn't want in your Wranglers?"

"Jealous?" I waggle my brows.

"Not in the least. There's only one woman I've truly ever wanted, and I'm making her my wife and off-limits to guys like you."

"I didn't know you thought so highly of me." I hang my head.

"Outside of your relationship with women, I think the world of you. You'd be a great husband and father if some woman could heal that heart of yours."

Why does my mind flash to Thayer? "You should get home before Kat sends out a missing person alert to the sheriff." I laugh, smacking him on the back. "Thanks for hanging out with me before you tie the knot."

"I'm here if you need me, no matter if I have a ring on my finger or not. You know that, right?" His jaw rocks back and forth.

"Thanks. There's nothing to worry about. Jace does enough of that, and I'm sure he'll oblige when he gets here."

"Good night. I'll see you on Saturday." He shuffles off to his truck.

As I'm unlocking my Bronco, I see Thayer walking along the side of the building, talking on her phone. Get in your vehicle, I tell myself but lose the inner battle as soon as I see her hang up the phone.

"Is everything alright?" I try a different approach.

She tugs her jean jacket closed. "Yeah."

"You have a beautiful voice."

"Um, thanks," she hums.

"Did your friend ditch you for some dude? I could give you a ride home."

"No. I'm good. I just needed some fresh air."

"We could go back inside, and I could buy you a drink." My cock notices when she draws her pink lip between her teeth.

"I don't think that's such a good idea." Her gaze falls to the ground.

"Sage told you to stay away from me, didn't she?"

"It's the whole bad boy thing." She twists her mouth.

"There's more to me than my reputation."

"I'm sure there is, but I'm not interested. I'm not your type."

"I wasn't aware you knew my type," I smirk.

"Look. I'm a city girl trying to settle into a town and style I'm not familiar with, and I prefer to do it on my own terms."

Any man that wasn't dead below the waist would consider her his type. "Have it your way, but it's too bad because I'd really like to get to know more about you," my voice echoes down the street. I tilt my Stetson and walk backward a few feet before I turn around. I'm in unfamiliar territory myself. I've never had a woman turn me down. It's a blow to my ego, making me want her more.

I turn up the radio, trying to cancel out the sound of her voice floating around in my head. Parking outside the garage at the main house, I stomp through the grass to the back door, and when I swing it open, Jace comes racing in my direction.

"It's about darn time you got home."

"What are you doing here? I thought you weren't due in until next week?"

"Plans changed when Walker moved his wedding date. I flew in with his parents."

"It's so good to see you, man." I hug him. "Did you get settled in a room upstairs?"

"Yeah, River told me to take Walker's room since he wouldn't be needing it anymore. I can't believe he and Katherine are getting married after all this time. Funny how life works out."

"He's the happiest I've ever seen him, and he's a great dad. Miller has fit in with everyone so well. It's like he's always been a part of our family."

"I met him, but only briefly before his grandparents swept him away."

"They'll spoil him rotten." I laugh. "Do you want a beer?" I mosey to the fridge.

"Why not." He snatches a bottle from my hand.

The living room is empty. "Where is everyone?"

"River and Greer are upstairs with the twins."

"It seems like yesterday this place was brimming with people. Mercy met Hardin, God love him," I snort. "Then Chase married Atley. Knox, who I never thought would fall in love, hooked up with Beck. And now, Walker's gone too."

He falls onto the couch and props his feet on the coffee table. "Sounds like a trend. Perhaps it's your turn."

"I'll pass that torch to you," I scoff. "I'm not the settling down type of cowboy."

"I don't know. My mother has always preached it happens when you least expect it."

My inhalation fills the room.

"How are you really? I know this day is always tough for you."

"It's just another day, man." I scratch my cheek.

"I know you better than anyone, and I wish the darkness in your eyes would disappear. Are you taking the meds?"

I glance over my shoulder, looking at the stairs. "Keep it down, Jace. You're the only one who knows I'm taking anything."

"That didn't answer my question."

"I take it when I need it."

"That's not how it works."

"You sound like my therapist," I huff.

"I've seen you at your lowest. I don't want to have to revive you again. That was the scariest day of my life when I found you on the floor of the garage. You have to keep holding on. As much as it feels like it, the pain you're feeling won't last forever. I don't claim to have the answers, but you need something to believe in and know that you're not alone. There's always a light at the end of the tunnel, and I feel it in my bones your time is coming."

"I know. And I am sorry, but I've never let my depression get that far out of control again. I'm good. I promise," I say, rocking back against the couch. "What are your plans? You never told me what made you decide to leave Salt Lick."

"Let's just say things weren't panning out for me there. River is going to have me work with Hardin part-time while I become a fireman."

"That's great. You've talked about it for years but never acted on it."

"Chase pulled some strings and got me into the program."

"It does help having a cousin as the sheriff. How do your parents feel about it?"

"They were disappointed I didn't want to stay on the ranch, but Deacon was madder than an old wet hen.

It's left him to pick up the slack, and he wants something more too."

"I'm sure given time, he'll find a way to come out to Montana too. I know that's his goal."

He covers his yawn with his hand. "It's late, and I'm exhausted." He hops up. "We'll finish catching up in the morning. Are you sure you're good?"

"Stop worrying about me. You'll want to get up early. Mercy makes a mean breakfast for the men, and if you sleep in, you'll miss out."

"Thanks for the heads-up. I'll set my alarm. Good night." He hustles up the stairs.

I take my time, finish my beer, and head to the shower before climbing into bed. The sheets get tangled between my legs as I wrestle with falling asleep. Jace is right; this day always haunts me more than others, and I fight the sadness that's seated in my heart. Rachel found her peace but left me tormented and alone. Every time I close my eyes at night, I see her face, but tonight I see the new stranger in town, and it gives me hope even though she shot me down. Her face blurs, and Rachel's reappears. Sleep evades me to the point I finally give up and get out of bed. Grabbing the bottle of pills, I down one, then get dressed and walk through the dark house, out the back door to the garage where I feel most in control.

Dragging out my toolbox, I set out to fix one of the tractors that Hardin broke.

"Couldn't sleep?" Mercy's voice startles me.

"Damn, is it morning already?"

"Yeah. I saw the light on out here and knew it would be you." She leans against one of the work benches. "What demons are keeping you up at night?"

"Same ones that never leave." I sigh.

"You let them control you too much."

"How do you figure?"

"They are living in that space between your ears, and you're allowing them to stay as tenants. Kick their asses out once and for all."

My chin falls to my chest. "I wish I knew how to do that."

"You're a smart man, Blaise. There isn't any machine you can't fix. Think of your brain as a machine. What's broken, and what do you need to repair it?"

"I thought time, but I was wrong."

"Time only gives you distance. It doesn't heal you. My best advice is to find a woman you can trust unwaveringly. But she has to be able to expect the same from you. This is how we were raised and how our parents made their marriages work."

I lift my head and look at her. "When did you get so wise?"

"I've learned a lot from Hardin about demons and healing." She pushes off the bench. "When you fix the part that's broken, those demons of yours will go running faster than their feet can carry them."

My gaze shifts to her belly. "How are you feeling these days?"

"Six months pregnant and like a whale already." She laughs. "But I can't wait to meet this little one." She holds her hand on her stomach.

"I'm happy for the two of you."

"Happy is good, but faking a smile ain't. Fix it. I'll see you at the breakfast table," she says over her shoulder, heading out of the garage.

"Fix what's broken," I mutter.

4

THAYER

My heart has never hummed so sporadically at the sight of a man. "He's trouble, and that's the last thing I need," I whisper into the night air, watching him drive out of the parking lot.

"There you are. Are you coming back inside?" Sage marches down the sidewalk toward me.

"If it's alright with you, I think I'd like to call it a night. I have a few words I need to jot down before I turn in so that I don't get behind on my schedule."

"Sure. Whatever you want." She digs the keys from her purse and hits the remote, unlocking the car.

"That was so much fun. We'll have to go every karaoke night, and maybe next time, you'll meet the man of your dreams."

Those bright green eyes are what my body is aching for at the moment. What I'd give to be the only woman getting lost in them. How can I even think that? The only thing I know about him, other than he has a body to die for, is that he's a player. I've been so vulnerable because of my previous choices that I can't allow the craving I feel to overrun my good senses. I won't be a victim again, not even if I have to remain celibate. *A girl can never have too many toys.*

"The ride home wasn't long, but you were quiet. You okay?"

I zoom by her into the kitchen to grab a bottle of water to take to my room. "For some reason, that guy is stuck in my head."

"Who? Blaise?" She narrows her gaze. "Please tell me no. The one person in this town I'd steer clear of you're smitten with."

"I wouldn't say smitten." The corners of my mouth turn downward. "He did look mighty fine in those jeans."

She walks behind me, grasping my shoulders and moving me. "Go to your room and use whatever toys you need to, but get him out of your head. I'll put my earbuds on, and you can moan at the top of your lungs."

"Sage!" I howl.

"Better yet, because it will save my ears, write a dirty scene in your book with your leading character's face in mind." She shoves me through my bedroom door and slams it. "I meant it!" she hollers.

Changing into my pajamas, I pick up my laptop and rest against the headboard and place it in my lap. "Think about my character she says." My fingers tap the keyboard, and my male character's eyes morph to bright green.

"Stop it!" I shake the visual of him from my head and type again. Then I type his name wrong, and it becomes Blaise. "Damn it!" I slam my laptop shut, toss it on my nightstand, and turn off the light, lying on my side and curling up with my pillow.

I lie completely still, hoping that sleep will take over, but it only makes me needier. My fingers find the small purple vibrator stored in my bedside table, and I roll to my back and place my hand between my thighs.

"Are you sure you have the cowboy out of your system? I don't want to have to worry about you today while I'm taking photos of the wedding."

"Yes. I'm positive."

"I'm glad you came with me. I think you'll love this place." We get out of the car, and she opens the trunk, hauling out her gear. Slinging one of her bags over my shoulder, we walk inside a beautifully decorated barn.

"Wow! This is amazing." There are white lights strewn from the ceiling and candles in every nook and cranny. White flowers are tied to the rows of folding chairs, and a large wooden cross is at the altar with the double barn doors open behind it, bringing in a brilliant light.

"Hi, Katherine," I hear Sage say behind me. "I want

you to meet my best friend, who just moved here from Boston. I hope you don't mind that I made her my plus one today."

"Not at all." Her smile and beauty could light up this room all by themselves.

I shake her extended hand. "Thayer. I love how you decorated the barn."

"Thanks, and I love your name. Very unusual."

"It was my great-grandmother's last name. I met the groom at the brewery a couple of nights ago. He was very sweet. Congratulations."

"She'll have to tell you their story sometime. It's one you could write in your romance books," Sage says while setting up her equipment.

"You're an author? I love to read. You'll have to send me a link to find your books. Wait... you're not Thayer Hawkins?"

"That's me." I grin.

"I love your books, and they are oh so sexy." Her cheeks turn pink.

"They are heated," Sage hollers with a laugh.

"I'll have to have you sign my copy. Another day, of course. When we get back from our honeymoon, I'd love to have you over for dinner."

"That's sweet, thank you. And I'd like to hear yours and Walker's love story."

She lifts her wrist, glancing at her watch. "Oh, I gotta go. Mercy will kill me if I don't get ready in time." She spins on her heel. "I was serious about dinner," she tosses over her shoulder.

People start coming in, and I assume they are family members based on the quaint setting. I feel out of place. "I'm going to step outside and check out the rest of the place," I tell Sage, and she waves me off. I make the mistake of keeping my head down when I barrel out of the barn and run into the arms of a man.

"I'm so sorry. I should've been paying attention." I gaze up.

"It's not every day a beautiful woman lands in my arms." He smiles from ear to ear. "My name is Jace. My cousin is the groom."

"I'm Thayer. I'm here with the photographer." I point.

"Oh." He clears his throat when he sees her.

"Not *with her* with her," I clarify. "She's my best friend. I'm new to town and don't know anyone, so she thought this would be a good place to start."

"We have that in common. I just arrived this week and plan on staying." As he speaks, his focus stays on Sage. "She might just be the prettiest thing I've ever seen."

"I'll introduce you afterwards if you'd like."

"I would." His smile broadens.

"I see you've met the woman of my dreams." A firm hand slaps Jace's back, and I choke on my next breath.

Blaise is wearing a black suit with a silky green tie that matches his eye color. All sorts of dirty thoughts hit my brain as to what the characters in my book might use a tie like that. And I itch to brush the piece of hair that's fallen out of place on his forehead. Instead, I grip my dress at the hip.

"You look gorgeous," he says with an appreciative sweep of my body. "Baby blue is most certainly your color."

"I'm going to head inside," Jace says, uncomfortably tugging at his collar. "Don't forget your offer to introduce me to your friend later."

"I won't. It was nice to meet you, and again, I'm sorry for bumping into you."

"I didn't know you were going to be here today." Blaise's hand finds the small of my back, and I take a step back.

"Why would you have known? You and I only briefly met the other day." The sweet scent of his cologne is as intoxicating as he is, and I can't deny the impalpable current surging between us. It claws at places it shouldn't.

He grins and stuffs one hand in his pocket like he's preventing himself from touching me. "Fair enough. What do you say you join me after the wedding? There's a reception set up by the river. Have you ever ridden a horse?"

Is he asking me figuratively, or is he talking about his anatomy? "Excuse me?"

He tilts his head back, laughing. "I know you're from the city, but you do know what a horse is, right?"

"Of course I do." My cheeks heat up.

His gaze grows narrow and heated. "What did you think I was referring to?"

"What does a horse have to do with this conversation?" I play it off.

"To get to the reception, you have to ride a horse."

"Oh...I, um, I guess I won't be going."

"You can ride with me, and we can get to know one another."

I should say no. "Alright." *Damn it, libido.*

"Great. I'll see you after the wedding then." He bends down, kissing me on the cheek. "Sorry, I couldn't resist," he whispers in my ear, but somehow, I don't think he's one bit shameful.

Once the guests have arrived, I find an empty seat in the back and watch the wedding unfold. Katherine is a beautiful bride, and the look on Walker's face when she walks down the aisle is storybook-worthy. They share their written vows, and I hear a sob in the front row from a pretty olive-skinned woman with silver hair and strands of black peering through it. I can only assume it's the groom's mother because I see the resemblance of Walker in the man sitting next to her from his profile.

They exchange rings and are pronounced man and wife. They walk down the aisle, and he hugs a woman. I hear him call her sis. He takes a young boy by the hand, and the three of them walk out together as one happy family.

Sage makes her way around, snapping pictures, and stops to let me know she'll be busy for a while with the bride and groom.

"I'll be fine. Do what you need to do, and don't worry about me," I tell her. As soon as she steps outside, Blaise approaches me.

"That was an elegant wedding. Are all these guests family?"

"They are. We're a close-knit one. There's still a bunch that weren't able to make it. It's hard to get away from a ranch."

"So they don't live here?"

"No. We're all from Kentucky."

"I'd love to hear how you and your cousins ended up in Montana."

He extends his elbow toward me. "And I'll be happy to tell you." He leads me out of the barn, and we pass by a group of horses already saddled and waiting for their riders.

"We're not going to take one of those?"

"Nope. I want us to ride my horse." He holds open the stable door. "He's in the first stall on the right."

A pure black stallion sticks his head out when I click my heels toward him. "He's magnificent. What's his name?"

"Tornado."

I bust out laughing. "Wasn't that Zorro's horse?"

"Ah, I see you were a fan." Pure merriment beams on his handsome face.

"Does that mean you are the righter of wrongs?" I can't help but snort.

"I'll fight the good fight, my lady." He takes a bow, and I find him totally charming. No wonder he has all the ladies eating out of his hand.

I glance down at my dress. "I'm not sure this is the best outfit to be riding on a horse."

He opens the stall door and picks up a saddle, fastening it on the horse. "If you'd prefer, you could ride naked, but I couldn't promise that we would make it to our destination."

"Okay, cowboy. I'll be keeping my clothes intact," I smirk, but at the same time, feel warmth between my legs.

"It's probably best if you ride sidesaddle." He helps me up, but not without copping a feel of my ass. "Sorry, my hand slipped." He chuckles.

"Don't let it happen again," I retort. Please let it happen again, my girlie parts scream.

As we ride, he points out different things on the property. It's full of rolling hills yet plenty of flat land for cattle, with a stream running through it. It's so different from the hustle and bustle of Boston. Large buildings block your views, and you can't see any of the skyline.

"I bet the stars light up the sky at night." My head is slanted upward.

"Stick around until the end, and you'll find out."

He halts the horse and helps me down. We arrive at a covered area down by a wide part of the river.

Twinkling lights hang from the large trees. There are round tables decorated with white tablecloths, and each one boasts small dainty yellow flowers tied in bows with candles in the center. A makeshift dance floor sits out over the water with a DJ stand.

"This has to be the coolest thing I've ever witnessed. They don't do receptions like this in the city."

He walks beside me with his hand on the small of my back, and I let him this time. "I'll introduce you to my family."

5

BLAISE

The most beautiful girl in the world is on my arm. She makes my skin tingle every time I touch her, not to mention what she does to my dick. Her hand fits perfectly snug against my arm as I make the introductions to my family.

"I see you took me seriously when I told you to stay clear of her until after the wedding," Walker speaks in a low voice close to my ear. Taking a few steps to the side, I get him to follow me so Thayer can't hear us, leaving her with Knox, which might be a bigger mistake.

"She's different than the other women." I mess up my hair with one sweep of my hand.

"You don't even know her. What makes her any less a target for your libido than anyone else you've slept with?"

"I don't know. I just feel it in my bones."

"In your bone, or in your bones?" He chuckles with a grunt.

"I want her to be different." I lift a shoulder toward my ear.

He cuts his gaze to her. "She is beautiful."

"That smile of hers slays me." I lay my hand over my heart. "I think she just might be the pill that I need to get on with my life."

He firmly clasps my shoulder. "Go slow, and for Pete's sake, keep your damn jeans zipped. Let her make the first move."

"Is that what you did with Kat?"

"Hell no!" He laughs hard. "But our situation was not the same. I knew her, and we had a past."

"But look at her in that baby blue dress. How am I supposed to keep my hands off of her?"

"What's the harm in waiting? Knowing you, once you've gotten what you wanted, you won't be interested anymore.'"

I blow out a long breath. "You're probably right. I can't seem to feel anything for any woman."

"I'm not trying to cut you off at the knees. I want you to be happy and find someone to grow old with. Just go easy, and more importantly, don't ruin my wedding day."

"Alright, you win. I'll be a complete gentleman."

"With that wild heart of yours, I'm not sure that's possible." He smirks and ambles off to his bride.

"Everything alright?" Thayer touches my forearm, and it tingles again. "You were smiling, and now you look lost."

"Nothing for you to worry about. What do you say to a dance?"

"I don't know how to dance to this music." Her nose scrunches as she peers at the dance floor.

"I'm a good teacher, and I bet you're a quick learner." I extend my hand.

She squints for a brief second then her face lights up. "I'm sure you are." She locks her fingers with mine, and I lead her to the dance floor, where Chase and Atley are engrossed in a two-step.

We walk into the middle, and she faces me. My hands fall on her hips, and she looks at them. "Um... I don't see anyone else dancing like this."

"Their partners aren't as pretty as mine."

She laughs and removes my hands. "Are you going to teach me, or do I need to find some other cowboy to lead?"

"Like hell you are. I'll show you a few moves, and then you can follow." She picks the moves up easily, and we're swaying around the dance floor with the others. My smile slips when I see Sage glaring at us with her arms crossed over her chest. "Your friend doesn't look pleased."

Thayer searches for her and then shrugs. "She'll get over it." She waves her off with a fling of her hand.

"She really doesn't like me, does she?"

"In her eyes, you're nothing but trouble for me."

"Is that what you think too?"

"Absolutely." She grins. "That's why we're not going to be any more than friends and not the kind with benefits."

The music slows, and I draw her into me. "I can't say I'm not disappointed, but I'd still like to get to know you. What was it like living in Boston?"

"The opposite of this," she snorts. "Hustle, bustle, horns blowing, not a blade of grass in sight, much less cattle or horses."

"That sounds completely awful." I chuckle. "Why did you leave?"

She hesitates, biting the inside of her cheek. "I wanted to experience something more for my career."

"And what is it that you do? I know you have a beautiful voice."

"I'm an author."

We continue to sway to the music. "Fiction or nonfiction?"

"Fiction."

"Please don't tell me you're a romance writer?"

She quits moving. "I am." Her chin goes in the air.

Damn, she's killing me. Her appearance is innocent, but I bet she's wild on the inside. "It's just that you seem—"

"Like a prude?" Her brows raise.

"No. That's not where I was going with it. I'm sorry. I'm completely messing this up." I take her hand and lead her over to one of the tables that's empty at the moment. "I'd love to hear more about it."

She sits and stares at me. "What is it that you do? By the look of your hands, I'd say you work hard."

I raise my fingers in front of me. "It's a downfall of my trade. I'm a mechanic. There isn't any beast I can't fix."

"So, I can assume you're rather boring?" Her nails drum on the table. "Wild on the outside, boring on the inside."

I know she's making a point, but she's not far from the truth. I'm not boring but dead on the inside, that is, until she sparked my interest. "Alright, I'm an ass.

Can we start over? Because I'm dying to know who you are. Tell me something no one else knows about you."

"Why would I do that? Is this your approach with women? You feign interest until you get what you want from them?"

Ouch. Okay, maybe up until this point, I was incapable of anything more, always singular in the thought of how to get in a girl's pants and fuck them senseless. She's different. Yes, I undoubtedly want to get tangled in the sheets with this gorgeous lass, but in this moment, I want more.

"I'll make a deal with you. I'll keep my hands tucked in my pockets anytime I'm close to you so you don't think I'm trying to flip up the hem of your skirt."

"So you don't want what's under my dress?" She scowls.

"I didn't say that. My cock would have to be broken not to want a woman that looks like you, but I'll restrain myself in order to get to know you so you can see that I'm not a complete dog." The player in me wants to drag her into my arms and press her back against one of these old trees and drive into her as hard as I can. But I want to show her I can be more.

She shifts her shoulders and bites the corner of her lip before a smile plays on the corner of her mouth. "I sleep with a baby blanket my mother knitted for me."

I scratch my head. "What?'

"You asked me to tell you something no one else knew about me." Her gaze rocks back and forth with mine as if she's waiting for me to mock her.

"I think that's sweet."

Her smile fades. "She died when I was six, and I've slept with it ever since. It's the only thing that makes me feel close to her."

I place my hand over hers. "I'm so sorry."

She exhales. "It was a long time ago. She died of breast cancer."

"Is your father still alive?"

"Yes. He's retired military, still living in Massachusetts."

"Did he ever remarry?"

She shakes her head. "He said he only had three loves in his life, my mom, me, and his career. He's an amazing man, and I love him dearly."

"I'm glad you have him."

Her gaze snaps to mine. "I'm sorry. All that was a downer. I'm not sure why I told you any of that."

"Don't be sorry. I'm glad you did. Besides, I did ask."

"Turnabout is fair play. What's your deep, dark secret?"

"I don't have any. I'm an open book." *Other than I see a shrink, take medication to control my depression and the only girl I ever loved committed suicide, screwing me up for a lifetime.*

"I'm sure that's not true." She tosses her head back, laughing. "You forget, I write characters like you, and they all have something they're hiding before they get the woman they want."

"Then you have an unfair advantage of a creative mind." I stand. "The sun is starting to set. Do you want to watch the fireworks with me?"

"There are fireworks?"

"Yep. River is going to light up this ranch in celebration, but if we get there before they go off, you can peer up at those stars we were talking about."

She gets to her feet, and like I promised, I tuck my hands in my pockets until we reach my horse. I take a blanket out of his side saddle, and we walk down by the river away from the crowd of people, including the prying eyes of Sage.

"Your friend is very protective of you," I mention, laying out the blanket on the grassy bank.

"That works both ways. We've been through a lot together."

"I take it by your choice of karaoke songs I'd better not piss her off when it comes to you," I tease, and she howls.

"I should totally use that in a book."

"Oh great. I'll have to be careful what I do and say." She sits on the blanket, and I join her, shifting close but not touching her even though I'm aching to do so.

"Why aren't you a professional singer?"

"I enjoy writing more. In fact, I've even written a few songs for some up-and-coming artists, but there's nothing like building characters out of nothing more than thoughts and making them come alive and believing that readers are going to fall madly in love with them."

"You said you needed another venue for your writing. Does that mean you've only moved to Missoula temporarily?"

"There were other reasons, but I intend on staying."

"Care to share those other reasons now that I know you sleep with a blankie," I wisecrack.

"If you tell anyone, what the Dixie Chicks did to Earl will be mild." Pure merriment waltzes in her eyes.

"My lips are sealed." Speaking of lips, hers are edible. What I wouldn't give for a taste to see if it would spark any kind of emotion from me, but I made a promise not to touch her.

"Have you ever wanted to do anything other than be a mechanic?"

"I've never given it much thought. Walker's dad, Uncle Bear—"

"Wait. Is his name really Bear?" She grins.

"His real name is Bradley, but I don't think I've ever heard anyone call him that other than his wife when he's pissed her off. Anyway, I used to hang out with him in his garage from the time I was old enough to hold a wrench. I love to figure out how things work and how to fix them when they don't. I guess you could say I'm doing what I was born to do."

"You found your passion." She lies back, staring up at the sky. "These stars are truly amazing." She turns her head toward mine when I lie back, and my arm brushes against hers. "You're doing what you love, but deep in those green eyes of yours, there's pain."

I quickly look away.

"Who hurt you so badly that you're disconnected?"

"You're seeing things."

She rolls to her side. "I don't think so."

I'm saved from revealing any kind of emotion when the first firework lights up the night sky above us.

Pressing her lips together, she turns onto her back and watches the colors filling in around us as a light dusting of ash falls over us.

From the corner of my eye, I see her face glowing and the simple pleasure she has from watching. It's a beautiful thing to see. She's a danger to me...something I need...but can't have.

What is it about this man that makes me want to jump into his arms and be like every other woman in this town? The deep-seated sadness in his eyes has me longing to hold him, to find out his story, to heal whatever is broken inside him. For a split second, I wanted to kiss him, but a kiss to a player like him wouldn't be just a kiss. It would be like giving him the key to say, "Yes, I'll get in your bed."

Would sleeping with him be such a terrible thing? I could take all emotion out of it and just have a fling. He's not on the market for anything more than that. Would I be willing to risk it to be held in his arms for one night? The answer is no because I'm not that kind of girl. Hooking up with a guy for sex has never been my thing. I want the whole heart of the man and the wild, passionate sex that comes with it. Oh, I'm sure the man lying beside me on this blanket is all alpha male under the sheets with godlike, masterful skills that would leave me breathless and bruised.

Why does looking at him spark my arousal so much? Like a moth to a flame. I've been warned, and I don't need to borrow any more trouble, but the way he looks at me and shoots me that sexy smile makes me want to cook him breakfast every morning. *Stop it, Thayer.* You can't fix him, I admonish myself, shaking off the rest of my thoughts and enjoying the fireworks like I've never seen before over the countryside.

When they are over, he holds out his hand to help me off the ground, then wraps the blanket over my shoulders. All of the guests gather around, with Walker and his bride in the middle.

"I want to thank you all for being a part of this today. It was a long time coming, but I couldn't be happier. I was going through the motions of living my life, and I didn't wake up until Kat slammed back into my world. Not only did she give me my heart back, she added to it by bringing me a son." A boy walks into his arms, and everyone cheers.

"This overwhelming happiness I feel is what I wish for all of you." His gaze darts directly to Blaise, and more than ever, I want to know what he's hiding. "Take care of my boy as I sweep this beautiful woman off to our honeymoon."

"He'll be in good hands," Greer hollers.

He kisses his bride one more time, and they ride off on a horse together. It's like something out of a fairy tale or in one of my romance novels.

We walk back to our horse, and when Blaise leans down to lend me a hand up, instead of giving him my boot, I tilt his face to mine and softly kiss his lips. He stands tall, shoving his hands in his pockets, inclining his head toward mine for another kiss.

Before I lose all my good senses, I stop him, easing my hand on his chest. "I'm sorry. I got lost in the romance of the night."

A melancholy of sorts crinkles in the corners of his eyes, and he helps me onto the saddle. I can't help but touch my lips, thinking about our brief lip-lock. He tasted like desire if it were to have a flavor. We ride in silence in the crispness of the night.

He assists me in dismounting, and I hand him the blanket. "Thank you for the nice evening." He stands, gazing into my eyes like he wants to say something else.

"There you are. I've taken all the pictures I need, and I'm ready to go home," Sage interrupts, grasping my arm as if she's trying to drag me away from him.

Jace meanders up beside us. "You promised me an introduction," he states with a smile, removing his hat.

"This is my best friend, Sage," I tell him.

Sage rudely ignores him. "We really need to go."

"I'm sorry," I mouth the words to Jace and wave goodbye to Blaise before I walk to the car with her. "Why were you so rude back there?"

"Because I'm not interested in a roll in the hay."

"All he wanted was to meet you. You're making a judgment call based on what?" I snap, getting inside the car.

"I'm not interested, that's all, and neither should you be."

"Did you meet his family? They were all awesome, and Walker is a sweetheart."

"But Blaise isn't." She starts the engine and peels out of the driveway.

"How do you know that for sure? I loved our banter, and he was a complete gentleman."

"I've seen him around town, and I've heard stories about the hearts he's broken. I don't want you to be a notch on his belt."

"I know you're only trying to protect me, but maybe there's more to him than meets the eye."

"I highly doubt it," she scoffs with an eye roll.

My body twists in her direction. "Are you one of those girls whose heart he's broken? Because if you are, I'll help you stuff him in a trunk."

"No. I didn't sleep with him, if that's what you're asking." She cuts her gaze to me.

"Then what is it?"

She exhales. "Nothing. I just don't want you picking the wrong guy again."

"Admittedly, I don't have the best track record, but there's something about him that I want to get to know."

"Fine, but just know that I'll feed him to the fish if he hurts you." She aims a finger at me.

"And, what else?" I cross my arms over my chest.

"I'll apologize to Jace for my behavior."

"Good, because he didn't deserve it."

"Lord, I've missed my city-girl friend calling me out on my shit."

I think there is more to her story, but I know Sage, and she doesn't like to be pushed to share anything. When she's ready, she'll tell me what's really behind her bitterness toward me liking Blaise. I don't think it's directly related to him, but someone did something to hurt her.

After a quick shower, I fall into bed, physically exhausted yet unable to keep my mind from delving back into Blaise. Switching on the lamp, I take out the journal I keep in my nightstand to scribble down notes when an idea hits me for one of my books. My skin flushes in warmth as words leap onto the paper as I write with the same passion I felt tonight. When I'm done, I reread it several times and drop my hand between my legs, thinking solely of Blaise. He was so gorgeous in his attire, with his biceps bulging through his white button-down. His eyes, his full bottom lip, everything about him is showstopping sexy and charming.

My head falls back on the pillow, and I close my eyes, biting my bottom lip as my fingers find the perfect spot. My moan fills the room as I envision him pressing his chest against mine and nipping at my ear, urging me to come. My orgasm peaks quickly, but it's not satisfying and leaves me frustrated even more.

"Damn him for being in my head." I slam my journal into the drawer and turn off the light, lying on my side, forcing myself to fall asleep.

I wake to the sound of crunching. "It must have been a really good dream." Sage is sitting on the side of the bed, eating a bowl of Grape-Nuts cereal.

I blink my eyes to focus as I stretch, reaching for my phone. "What time is it?"

"Almost eleven in the morning," she chirps blissfully between the annoying crunch.

"Seriously." I jerk the tangled sheets from my legs and sit beside her. "I don't know how you eat that tasteless crap," I snap. "Why are you in my room watching me sleep?" I rake my hands through my knotted hair.

"I was worried about you and thought perhaps you'd been kidnapped or something. As long as I've known you, you've gotten up at the crack of dawn."

"I guess I was worn out. Is that a crime?" I nudge her with my shoulder.

"Well, if you'd have come in here and gone to bed rather than playing with your toys?" She laughs. "All that moaning kept me awake."

"I didn't play with my toys." I stand, red-faced.

"Yeah, whatever method you were using worked for you," she snorts and splashes milk from the side of her bowl when she gets to her feet.

"I need a new roommate," I chide. "This one is too nosy." I tilt my head upside down, letting my hair fall forward, and run a brush through it.

"Sorry, you're out of luck. I'm the only one willing to live with you. Besides, you love me, and you know it."

"Don't you have anything better to do than harass me?"

"Actually, I do. I've spent hours this morning developing the photos from last night. There's one, in particular, I want you to see."

I flip my long hair back and tie it in a messy bun. "Can I brush my teeth first?"

"I'll put on a fresh pot of coffee and wait for you in the kitchen." She saunters out.

Taking my dear sweet time, I wipe the makeup from my face leftover from last night and then not only brush my teeth but floss them too. Tugging on a pair of soft lounge pants and a gray T-shirt with no bra, because who needs one with just us girls living here, I head for the pot of coffee.

"It took you long enough," she snarks as she peruses her laptop and pours a cup of coffee for me.

"What's so important?" I toss in a dash of coconut sugar and heavy cream, then pull out the chair beside her.

She lays out a bunch of black-and-white photos in front of me.

"Wow, these turned out great. You have so much talent." I skim through them.

She grips another photo in her hand so that I can't see it. "This is the one I wanted to show you, and with your permission, I'd like to put it on a canvas to one day display in my gallery." She lays it down.

"This is really good, but what's so special about it? I mean, the others are just as good." My gaze is riveted to the photo of me and Blaise dancing. My head is slightly thrown back, and I'm laughing at something he said.

"The look he's giving you speaks volumes. I've never seen so much desire in a man's eyes. It's even seated in the fine wrinkles around them. His thirst for you leaps out of the photo."

I stare at it, and the warmth between my thighs returns. "Why would you want to share it if you've warned me away from him?" My words are soft as I drink in the sight of him.

"Because not even you could write the type of emotion playing on his face."

"I think you're being a little melodramatic." I scoff at her, but I totally see what she sees.

"Say what you will, but that's the face of a man who wants what's in front of him. It's the perfect example of why you should stay clear of him."

Pressing the coffee mug to my lips, I take a sip. "Let me get this straight. You see a man full of passion for me, and I should stay away from him? Why shouldn't I be sprinting to his bed?"

"Because he's a master of that look. It's why women want him."

"So, the look isn't really for me, is what you're saying." I shrug.

"Exactly. It's a tool he's perfected to woo you."

"Then I guess I'm blind because I completely missed it. I was too busy enjoying his company." I set my mug down a bit too hard. "Why do you think the worst of him?"

She plops against the back of her chair and drums her fingernails on the table. "Let's just say I'm all too familiar with his type."

"Did someone hurt you?"

"I don't want to talk about it." She stands abruptly. "Just please don't get ensnared in his game."

"I'm a grown woman who is fully capable of making decisions for myself, and I like him. That doesn't mean I'm going to jump in bed with him."

The doorbell ringing gets both of our attention. "Are you expecting someone?" Sage points to the door.

"No. I hardly know anyone in town. It has to be for you."

She peeks through the blinds. "Um, it's most definitely not for me."

I look around her to see out. "Blaise?" Completely forgetting I'm braless, I swing open the door.

His gaze drops to my bare feet, then skims upward, licking his lips. "I, um...brought you the best cinnamon rolls in town. Walker's new wife, Kat, makes them." His eyes darken as he holds the box out.

Crossing my arms over my chest, I become keenly aware of the nakedness under my T-shirt, and I shift my arms higher, trying to hide it. "How did you even know where I live?"

He's still staring. "My cousin Chase that you met last night is the sheriff, and he looked you up for me."

I should be angry, but when his lips turn into that gorgeous smile of his, butterflies tickle my insides, but a warning flashes through my brain at the same time. "He shouldn't have done that, and you shouldn't have asked him to. It's stalkerish." I nearly choke on my words.

His eyes fill with concern, and he takes a step back. "I'm sorry, I had no right to ask him. I just thought—"

"You thought what? Stalking a woman is okay?" My voice rises more than I mean it to, and Sage darts next to me.

"You need to leave her alone," she snaps.

The look on his face says it all. He's dumbfounded by my reaction when it appears to be an innocent, sweet move on his part. "I got this," I tell Sage, backing her down.

She directs two fingers toward him and then toward her eyes before she spins on her heels.

I lift the lid of the box and inhale. "These smell heavenly."

"I'm truly sorry. I didn't get your phone number, and I wanted to see you again." He hands me the box and then tucks his hands in his pockets.

"Would you like to come in and have one with me?"

His gaze slips from my eyes to my chest. "I don't think that's such a good idea. My resolve to not touch you is only so strong."

I gaze down. "I'll get dressed and meet you some-where...safe," I add.

"How about the bakery two blocks down where I purchased these." He hikes a thumb over his shoulder.

"Give me fifteen minutes, and I'll be there."

"Great." He grins, keeping his hands tucked away but stealing one more glance at my nipples protruding from underneath my T-shirt that feel harder by the moment. "I'll see you there." He shuffles off, and I shut the door.

"You're seriously going to meet him after what he just pulled?" Sage is tapping her foot on the floor.

"I really don't think he meant any harm."

"Have you not learned anything after the crap you went through with your last so-called boyfriend?"

Laying the rolls on the table, I turn to face her. "In fact, I have. I took self-defense classes and learned how to use a gun. I'm not going to live my life in fear or stick my head in the sand. I did that long enough. If I do, then he won all the power over me, and I'm not having it. I'll be cautious, but I'm not living like a nun. If I feel he's worth the risk, I'm going to take it."

She closes the gap between us and sweeps a strand of hair over my shoulder. "Okay. I only want you to be safe."

"I know you do, and I love you for it." I hug her. "And I will be."

7

BLAISE

"Smooth move scaring her, cowboy," I mutter, finding a table open by the window so I have a street view to see her when she arrives at the bakery. But damn, the sight of her braless has me even more on edge. Tampering down the physical reaction she ignites in me is going to be hard so I can take my time to get to know her.

"Hey, Blaise," a woman I hooked up with a few weeks ago says, standing at my table. "What do you say you come over to my place tonight?" Her hand brushes my cheek.

Any other time I would've taken her up on her offer to have meaningless sex. "I'll have to pass."

"How about a rain check?" She winks.

"I've met someone." I sit tall, not sure if I'm trying to convince her or myself that I have a chance with Thayer.

She leans close to my ear. "When you lose interest, or she can't satisfy that voracious need of yours, give me a call."

As she walks away, she stumbles into Thayer and apologizes for being distracted.

"A friend of yours, I assume," she coolly states, sitting. She's wearing the same gray T-shirt with it off one shoulder, exposing her bra strap, and a light-weight denim jacket over it paired with white pants. I can't help but wonder if she exposed the strap on purpose, but it does a number on my cock.

"I'm sorry," I say, folding my hands on the table.

"For which thing? Her?" She tilts her head in the direction of the woman on the sidewalk. "Or showing up at my place uninvited?"

"Both."

"Don't do it again. I have a gun, and I'm not afraid to use it."

I inhale sharply, squeezing my eyes shut, trying like hell not to envision her gripping a gun naked. "I won't. I promise, only with an invitation from you."

"That's not likely to happen unless you'd like Sage on your ass."

"She scares me a bit." I chuckle.

"She should." She finally smiles, and I know I'm forgiven.

"I thoroughly enjoyed spending time with you last night. You look good on a horse. You should come by the ranch, and I'll teach you to ride." The horse isn't the only thing I want her riding.

Stop.

Focus on her words.

Her words.

Not her lips.

Not her nipples.

Not the light in her eyes when she smiles, and damn sure not the way she looked in her baby blue dress.

She squints and bursts out laughing.

"What's so funny?" I picture my grin matching her dazzling smile.

"You're talking to yourself, aren't you? Your facial expressions gave you away. It's the exact same ones I'd give one of my characters in my books."

"You are way too observant, and I think I need to read one of these books of yours." I lean back casually, relishing her merriment at my expense.

"I don't believe I write the type of stories you'd want to read."

"I'm willing to try something new."

"Really?" She raises a single brow with a sexy tilt to it.

Is there anything this woman does I don't find alluring? Another woman walks by and winks at me.

"Are there any woman in this town you haven't slept with?"

There's that busting my chops thing again. "Yes, plenty." I clear my throat. A cowboy grins, tipping his hat at her as he walks by, and it stirs something primal in me. I want to yell, telling him she's off-limits and to keep his bug eyes to himself. An inexplicable need to claim her as mine settles in my chest. I really should see my therapist.

"It's not often I ask a woman out on a second date."

She shifts her head from side to side, furrowing her brow. "We haven't been on a first date."

"Technically, no, but last night should count. I mean, we got to lay on a blanket and watch the fireworks together."

"Funny, not the kind of first date I'd see you going on. Kinda more like wham-bam-thank you-ma'am."

"Wow, your friend must really hate me." I halfheartedly chuckle.

"I'm sorry. That was a little judgmental of me."

Resting my elbows on the table, I lock my hands together so I'm not tempted to run my thumb along her bottom lip. "What do you say you allow me to start over with a clean slate? Forget everything you've heard about me."

She twists her lips together as if she's contemplating the idea. "Alright. I'll give it a try."

I hold out my hand. "Hi. My name is Blaise Calhoun. It's very nice to meet you, Miss..."

She boasts a serious look, trying not to laugh. "Thayer Hawkins."

Even her name is foxy. "Miss Hawkins, from Boston, who writes romance, what else do you like to do?"

"If I were in the city, I'd say exploring galleries and museums, but here, I'd like to go shooting."

"You mentioned you have a gun."

"Yes. I took a few classes to get certified to carry, but I'd like to perfect my skills."

"I'd love to accommodate you on one condition."

"Let me guess...I don't use it on you when you show up at my door."

I tap my finger to my nose. "Or ever, for that matter."

"Then don't give me a reason to," she snickers.

Shifting in my seat, I tuck my hands in my pants. "I'm keeping these babies right here," I howl, and she blushes.

"Am I that tempting to you?"

"You have no idea." My jeans tighten in the crotch.

She peers away, and her tongue sweeps out over her bottom lip. "Blaise Calhoun from...Kentucky, if I remember right, who is a mechanic, and more than capable of riding a horse, what else to you like to do? Besides the obvious." She quirks a brow.

"Well, since you've cut me off of my favorite pastime" —I pout—"I'm a man that loves many things. The rodeo, fishing, farming, corralling cattle, shooting, and I'm planning on taking up reading in the very near future."

Her expression is full of amusement. "Charmer," she mutters.

"I'll take that as a compliment." I rap my knuckles on the table. "When do you want to go on this date?"

"I'm behind on my writing schedule. The move set me back, but I could go on Saturday."

"Tomorrow," I state.

"I didn't realize this was a negotiation. Friday." She cuts me a sharp look.

"Too long to wait. Today."

"Wait, you're going the wrong way in this negotiation," she hoots. "Wednesday at the earliest."

I inhale, scrunching my nose. "Do you have a cancellation list?"

She folds over in laughter. "This isn't a doctor's appointment."

"Surely you can fit me in between lunch and dinner somewhere in that busy schedule of yours."

"I'll give you one thing, you're persistent."

"Only when it's something I truly want."

She reaches for her purse and pulls out her phone, handing it to me. "Give me your number. I'll call you if I have any openings in my day."

I tap it in and hit dial, so I'll have her number. I hand it back to her, and she lights up, but not before typing in my contact name.

"The Charmer," she reads it. "Really?" She tucks it into her lap. "You do have a wild side, don't you?"

"Keep him wild, baby," I tease.

"I think you could use a little taming."

"I'm up for you being my trainer if you'd like."

She waves her phone at me. "You'd fire me in a minute. I'd be way too hard on you."

I rock forward and whisper, "You're already way too hard on me."

She stands, pushing her strap under her shirt. "I walked right into that one."

"Call me when you get that cancellation or if you miss me," I smirk with all the allure I can muster.

"I'll see you Wednesday." She skips out the door.

I watch her sway her hips down the sidewalk until I can no longer see her. I tap my phone and press it to my ear.

"I said Wednesday." I can hear her smiling.

"I miss you already. I love our banter."

"Goodbye, Charmer," she quips and disconnects the line.

Glancing at my watch, I hustle out and make my way down the block to the two-story building to the woman who knows all my dirty secrets.

"I didn't see you on the appointment book today," her secretary says, and I march past her.

"I'm not." I knock and then barge into her office. Evie is typing on her computer with her reading glasses perched on the end of her nose.

"I'm sorry, Dr. Shields..." her secretary says.

"It's alright. If he's showed up unannounced, it must be important."

She shuts the door behind me but not without giving me an angry bumblebee glare.

"Have a seat, Blaise." She shuts her computer and lays her glasses on the desk before she joins me in her usual spot. She sits, crossing her legs, then smiles at me. "That's a first," she scoffs.

"What?" I ask, confused.

"You didn't ogle my legs. Are you sick?"

She's right. I didn't pay any attention. I press the back of my hand to my forehead. "Maybe that's what's wrong with me. Do I look ill?"

"No." She laughs. "A little flustered but not sickly. What is it that has you in a tailspin?"

"I met this woman, and I can't stop thinking about her."

"Do tell," she says.

"She's the prettiest thing I've ever seen. A natural beauty and funny, but she likes to make jokes at my expense." I keep rambling. "Her best friend hates me and told her that I'm a player."

She lifts one shoulder. "You have been, and that's what best friends do. They warn you off of someone they don't think would be good for you."

"I deserve it." I slump to the couch.

"You're the only one who can change her opinion on that. My advice is if you're truly interested in this woman beyond sex, you need to win her friend over."

"Oh, believe me, I want to have sex with her."

"Tell me something."

"What?" My fingers fly through my hair.

"Have you kissed her yet? You've always told me when you kiss a woman, you feel nothing. Is she any different? Did she spark an emotion inside of you?"

"She is different because she kissed me first, and yes, I felt something in that sweet moment."

"Describe it to me."

My cheeks puff when I blow out air. "It stirred a desire not just to ravage her but to get to know the person behind the kiss. Her mind, her emotions, what drives her...."

"Not what sound she makes in bed?" She raises a brow to a comment I made a while ago.

"That, too, but so much more."

"I think you've finally made a breakthrough."

"But what if I screw it up by just being me?"

"You need to recall who you are on the inside. The man I've gotten to know is sweet and vulnerable. I think you'll find a man with a lust for life, not just for the opposite sex. The drive was taken away years ago, but shadows of him still exist, and you need to dig that out and run with it. Take it one day at a time."

"I know I should, but every part of me is bursting to jump in headfirst, but what if my heart doesn't follow?"

"Don't overanalyze it. Just let it develop."

I stand and start pacing. "It will end badly."

"Don't go there," she warns.

"Three months, six months at the most."

"Breathe, Blaise. Don't set an end date."

"I don't know how not to," I snap sharply out of frustration. "I won't let it start. That's how I prevent it." I stop pacing.

"How are you ever going to move on if you can't take a step forward?"

"Her friend was right in warning her. I'm not the man for her."

She gets to her feet, and steps in front of me with her hands braced on my shoulders. "Don't do this. Don't end it before you have a chance to heal your heart. I'll meet with you every day if that's what it takes to get you through this."

"You'd do that?"

"Yes. You call me, and I'll come to you. This is the breakthrough I've been waiting for you to have to move on."

"Alright. I'll keep my cool and you on speed dial."

8

THAYER

"You have an extra giddyup in your step, and you can't quit smiling. Tell me what happened." Sage drags me to the couch.

"I know you want me to stay away from Blaise, but I really like him, and I'm officially going on a date with him."

Her head droops. "I really wish you wouldn't."

"There's something about him I can't walk away from, and he's been completely hands-off. In fact, I'm the one that kissed him."

She lifts her head. "You kissed him?"

I draw my knees to my chest and hug them. "Yes." I feel my eyes grow fuzzy. "It was sweet and gentle, but the spark nearly burned me, and I want to do it again every time I'm near him."

She collapses against the back of the couch. "Please don't let him take advantage of you."

"I won't. I promise. If I ever feel uncomfortable, I have your phone number on speed dial."

"I'll make sure the shovel is in my trunk." She smirks. "Seriously, if this is what you want, I'll try and be supportive."

"Thank you, that's all I'm asking."

"When is this date?"

"Wednesday, if not earlier," I beam. "It was a negotiation on his part, and he wants to see me sooner, but..." I scamper to my feet. "I'm way behind on my deadlines, and I need to lock myself in my writing cave to catch up. If you haven't seen me by the end of the day, be sure to bring me food and water," I tease.

"You forget how well I know you. I stocked a box under your bed with protein bars and water."

"What do you have planned for the rest of your day?"

"I'm going to finish developing the wedding pictures, and I'm going to run them out to the ranch. Walker requested they be delivered before he gets back from his honeymoon."

"If you run into Blaise, please be nice." I wave a finger at her. "And don't forget you owe Jace an apology."

"I haven't forgotten," she mutters.

"Do you want to eat at the brewery tonight?"

"Yes, yes, and yes," she cheers. "I love going there."

"Alright, I'll plan on being ready by six." I walk into my bedroom and sit at the small desk Sage ordered for me as soon as I agreed to move to Montana. Opening my laptop, I find the file for my manuscript, and it doesn't take long for me to get lost in the story. My face feels warm and pink when my fingers fly into the sex scene. It's steamy and erotic like I've never written before, and I have to pull out a bottle of water from the box Sage stocked to cool my racing heart. I've only ever written about great sex before and never truly experienced that true lust for a man. Sex has been mediocre at best other than in my novels. I'm not sure it's not all fictional. Does a man really care about a woman's needs?

My bottom lip hurts from gnawing my teeth into it, fantasizing what it would be like to have Blaise's hands on my body, scorching my skin with every touch. Is that what it would really be like, or is it all in my head?

Shaking it off, I continue with my story until I hear a knock on my door.

"Thayer, are you still locked in your cave?"

I twist my neck to look at the time. "Crap." I hop to my feet and open the door. "I'm sorry. I lost all track of time. It'll take me five minutes to change clothes."

She follows me into my closet. "I knew you'd get caught up in your writing."

"Did you run out to the ranch?"

"No," she huffs. "A few of the pictures need adjustments. I want them to be perfect before I deliver them."

"How is this?" I hold up a silky light pink top with a pair of skinny jeans.

"We really need to work on your wardrobe," she snickers. "You're way too fancy. Don't you own anything plaid?" She scoots hangers looking through my tops.

"No, and I don't plan on it," I scoff, tugging off my T-shirt and buttoning the blouse.

"Suit yourself." She shrugs.

I squat, finding a pair of matching pink heels.

"Nothing says city girl like fancy shoes in a cowboy boot town." She laughs.

After I buckle them around my ankle, I snag her hand. "Come on, let's get out of here." I stop long enough to grab my purse and cell phone.

She gets behind the wheel, and I check my messages. My heart skips a beat when I see one from Blaise, a.k.a the Charmer.

Blaise: *Did you get a cancellation? I can't wait to see you again.*

Me: Barely time to eat and drink. You were my inspiration and I got lost in my character.

I don't expect such a quick response but smile when I see the three dots, and I find myself holding my breath, waiting.

Blaise: I was your muse. That means your character is a sexy as sin alpha male that will ultimately win the beautiful woman from Boston.

Me: It's fiction, remember? There was no girl from Boston in my story.

Blaise: There is in mine. What are you wearing?

Me: What happened to you being a gentleman?

Blaise: That's only in person. I can fantasize just like you do in your books. Do you have on a pink bra?

My chin falls to my chest, peeking between the buttons. How did he know?

. . .

Me: ... I'm totally blank.

Blaise: You are aren't you? LOL

Me: I'm sure you'd like to know but I'm not going to tell you.

Blaise: Pink it is.

Me: Leave me alone. I include a laughing emoji.

Blaise: What are you doing tonight?

Me: *Going out to dinner with Sage.*

Blaise: Have fun.

I'm disappointed he didn't ask me where. I fold the phone in my lap.

"You really do like him, don't you?" Sage takes her gaze off the road and grins.

"More than I should for a man I hardly know," I admit.

She parks, and the place isn't busy like it was on karaoke night, but there is still a substantial crowd. We're seated in a booth in the bar area, and we order mango margaritas along with bottomless chips and salsa.

"I do believe these are the best margaritas I've ever had." I lick the sugar from the rim.

"Wait until you have their steak fajitas." She rubs her belly. "You've not tasted anything so good in your life."

"This town is quickly growing on me."

Sage's eyes narrow, and she scoots out of the booth. "Are you stalking her?" Her voice is loud and angry.

I wheel around to see who she's talking to, and it's Blaise. Jace is behind him.

He scowls. "No. We come here all the time for dinner." His inflection sounds as aggravated as hers.

I stand and grab her hand. "It's alright, Sage. Calm down."

"Calm down," she shrieks, tossing my words back at me. "You don't need another boyfriend stalking you."

She follows me when I jerk her away. "Stop it. He isn't, nor does everyone in this restaurant need to know anything about my past, and I'd appreciate it if you'd keep your voice down." My words come out between gritted teeth. "I should be the one that's paranoid, not you."

She blows out an exhale. "I'm sorry, you're right. It's a small town, and we're bound to run into him." She takes my hand and spins me back around. "I'm sorry. I don't know what I was thinking."

"It's all good," Blaise says, but he can't hide the concern in his eyes. "You had a stalker?" His tone is low and menacing.

"Since we're all here, why don't you two join us for dinner?" I have to veer him from this conversation that I'm not ready to have with anyone.

Jace removes his Stetson. "I'd like that."

Grasping his arm, I have him sit in the booth with me, and Blaise slides in across from me.

"Besides, my dear sweet friend has something to say to you." My teeth gnash in a fake smile.

"Yes, she's right. I want to apologize for being rude to you after the wedding. I was out of line. I get a tad bit carried away when it comes to Thayer." She pinches her fingers together, leaving a small gap.

"I'll forgive you if you allow me to buy you another one of those drinks." Jace points to the margarita glass, grinning.

"Shouldn't it be the other way around?" she snorts.

"Fine, I'll let you buy me a beer." His smile is infectious, spreading to Sage.

Glancing at Blaise, his eyes are downward, and his hands are clasped together. His silence has me worried. "So, I guess you win. You got to see me before Wednesday," I try to tease him, but he's not having it. The intensity in his jawline says it all.

I call out for the waitress when she walks by. "I understand this place has the best fajitas."

"Yes, ma'am."

"I'll take an order of them."

"Me too," Sage pipes in.

"Make it three," Jace says.

Blaise holds up four fingers.

"Two beers," Sage adds.

"Bud Light," Jace tells her.

Sage and Jace converse easily back and forth, and Blaise keeps his gaze on his lap. Lifting my foot, I touch his shin to get his attention. "You look nice."

He flattens his lips and nods. "Thanks. You look beautiful in your pink blouse." He emphasizes the color, and I'm sure my cheeks match it.

He lightens up a bit, but I can tell he has a million questions running through his mind. As much as I'm not ready to talk about it, Sage has put it out there, and I don't think Blaise is the type of man to let it go.

9

BLAISE

No wonder she was aggravated that I showed up at her house. I really did scare the shit out of her, and that's why Sage has her nose out of joint. I'd never in a million years harm her or any woman for that matter. Coming on strong won't work for a woman like her. I'll need to back off, but if I ever get my hands on her stalker, lord help him.

Sitting across from her is killing me. I want to hold her and let her know I'd protect her with my life. Rocking my head from side to side, I attempt to relieve the tension and focus on Thayer. She's damn pretty, and I think pink is my new favorite color.

Our food comes, and we keep the conversation light. Jace and Sage seem to have made friends, and then I recall what my shrink advised.

"How did the wedding pictures turn out." I angle toward her.

"Really good. There are a few that I need to adjust."

"How long have you been a photographer?"

"My father bought me a camera when I was five years old, and I've toyed with them ever since. I'd say a camera was my best friend until I met Thayer."

"You're from here. How did you end up on the East Coast?"

"I was a military brat, and we moved all over until we settled in Boston. It was the longest I had lived anywhere. I'm very thankful I had the opportunity to spend my high school years with Thayer, but I left as soon as she moved on to college."

"You two have obviously stayed in touch."

"Every day." She smiles at Thayer.

"I apologize if I've made you uncomfortable. It wasn't my intention, and you need to know that I'd never hurt her."

"It's a start"—she shrugs—"but your reputation proceeds you in this town."

"I'm very well aware, and it's time I made amends and grew up. We all have ghosts, Sage." I briefly gaze at Thayer and then back at her.

"Yes, we do." She sighs.

"I'd like to start over with you as well."

She twists her torso toward me. "A clean slate?"

"Yes. A do-over."

Her brow narrows. "You only get one do-over with me. If you hurt her..."

"I know." I laugh. "I'll have the same fate as Earl." I offer her my hand, and she shakes it.

"As long as we have an understanding."

"Yes, ma'am." I smile.

This is one of those days that I'm happy, as opposed to days it's hard to breathe, barely holding on. It's a good feeling. This seems ordinary, something I haven't felt in forever.

A discreet yawn leaves Thayer's lips, and she tries to hide it. "I can take you home if you'd like."

"No, I'm good." She waves me off but yawns again.

"I'm not ready to go home," Sage orders another drink.

"I really don't mind giving you a ride home," I say again.

"I'll hang out here if that's alright with you." Jace tips his bottle to Sage's glass.

"Are you good with that? I really am tired." She waits for Sage to respond.

"I better not wake up to you at my breakfast table in the morning." She faces me, and the corner of her lip curls.

"Sage!" Thayer admonishes her. "I'm more than capable of making my own decisions."

She stands, letting me out. "I'm only teasing. I agreed to give him a chance." She gets close to my ear. "But remember what I told you," she whispers.

I nod and chuckle. "Will do. I'll leave you in good hands with Jace."

Thayer slides out of the booth and lays her hand on my arm, and we make our way out together. I open the truck door for her and trot to the other side.

"Thanks for being friendly to Sage. She comes across as stern, but once you get past all her gruffness, she's really sweet. She hasn't had the easiest life, and she's determined to protect the people she loves. Our fathers were stationed at the same base. I was fortunate enough that my dad had a position where we didn't move around. If he got sent out, he'd be gone for a couple of months and then come back to Fort Devens, so I had a stable life. Sage didn't. The other thing we had in common was that we both lost our mothers at a young age."

"I can relate to that. My family is the same way. If you cross one of us, you cross us all. In the reverse circumstance, if one of us loves you, we all love you. I can't blame her for wanting to protect you."

I'm parking outside her house within minutes, and it's the first time I've been unsure if I should invite myself in or not. It's usually not a question.

"Do you want to come inside?"

Yes, and I want to hold you. "You're tired and should get some sleep."

She tilts her head. "I'm inviting you in, Blaise. It's okay to say yes, and you don't have to keep your hands tucked in your pockets." She doesn't wait for my response before she opens the door, and I have no intention of turning down her offer.

The keys rattle as she unlocks her door. It's a small two-bedroom rental house that's very tidy and decorated in orange colors, reminding me of the same color of the apricots we used to pick from the trees growing up. Black-and-white prints that I assume were taken by Sage line the walls in the living room.

"She has a lot of talent." I stand, admiring them.

"Her aspirations are to open her own gallery in town."

"I know the perfect place to get her started. Walker's wife Katherine remodeled one of the buildings on Main Street. She could rent one of the stations and display her artwork."

"That sounds perfect. I could rent it and surprise her with it. She's got one of those portable storage units in the backyard full of her artwork."

"What is she waiting for?"

"I think she's afraid to truly put herself out there in fear of failure."

"If you want, I could help set the space up for her."

"That's very sweet of you, and I'll take you up on your offer. Would you like a drink? I can make a pot of coffee if you'd like." She yawns.

My fingertips rub together before I raise my hand and cup her face. "We should get you to bed."

"I'm tired, but I don't want you to go yet." She leans into the palm of my hand for a brief moment, then takes it into hers and leads me into her bedroom. "I want to show you my writing cave, which also seconds as my bedroom," she tosses over her shoulder.

Her white down comforter looks inviting, but I ignore the draw it has on me. She has a small wooden oak desk, settled against a gray wall with a large bookshelf next to it.

"Are these all books you've written?" I run my hand down the spine of one of them.

"These three shelves, yes. The others are books written by my favorite authors."

"May I?" I ask, taking one down.

"You, um...probably won't like it." She snatches it from my hand and tosses it on the bed.

"Okay, how about this one?" I point.

She shakes her head and pinches her lips together.

I close the gap between us and stare into her eyes. "Are you concealing that you're as wild as I am, but you hide it behind words?"

Her tongue sweeps out over her bottom lip, and her gaze shifts to my mouth. "We all have a little bit of a naughty side in us."

My cock whips to life, wanting to know the extent of her naughtiness. Slowly, I lower my hand and kiss her, claiming her with every swipe of my tongue. The odd thing is, I think she's doing the same for me. This kiss isn't like anything I've ever experienced. Everything that I haven't let myself feel for years is wrapped up in it, and it's an affection I don't want to let go of.

We walk backward until her knees hit the side of the bed. "Blaise," she rasps with her warm breath permeating my lips. "I'm not ready for this. I don't want to be like every other woman to you."

"What do you want?" I press my forehead to hers, keeping my eyes locked on hers.

Her hand drops from my neck to my chest. "I want this," she whispers.

"Up until the day I laid eyes on you, I didn't think I was capable of giving anyone my heart, but you make me want so much more."

A wave of detachment comes between us when she drops her hand. "I won't be a one-night fix for you."

"I don't think one night with you would ever be enough for me. I'm willing to wait until you believe me."

"Thank you," she says and sits on the edge of the bed.

"I do need something from you." I join her and wrap my arm around her waist. "Tell me what happened to you."

"You mean my..." She sighs. "Can't you just forget Sage ever blurted that tidbit out?"

"Not going to happen."

She scoots to the middle of the bed and leans against the headboard. Kicking out of my boots, I mimic her position and cross my long legs at the ankle, waiting for her to start talking.

"I was a senior in high school when I published my first book under a pseudonym because I didn't think anyone would want to read a romance book written by an eighteen-year-old girl. I had no idea how well it would sell. My publisher set up a book signing at the biggest bookstore in Boston."

"That had to be exciting."

"It was and overwhelming. I had to give a synopsis of my book to the attendees, and there was this handsome man in the crowd that I found completely intriguing. He stayed afterward to meet me and asked me out on a date."

"You said man. How old was he?"

"The same age I am right now, twenty-five. By all appearances, he was someone who had his act together and was very likable, except—"

"Sage didn't like him," I finish her thought.

"She had a gut feeling about him, and I shut her down because I found him fascinating. I was very naive." She twists her hands into knots in her lap.

Reaching over, I peel them apart and take one in mine. "What happened?"

"I started seeing red flags with him. He'd come over unannounced and be angry if I hadn't responded to one of his texts as quickly as he thought I should. He'd show up at my high school and threaten any boy that would look in my direction. It was too much. His possessiveness turned me off."

"So you broke it off with him."

"I tried, but he wouldn't leave me alone. My father ended up filing a restraining order against him after he nearly beat down our door to get to me."

"Let me guess...that didn't deter him."

"I thought it had. He stopped calling me and sending me texts, and I hadn't seen him lurking around for a couple of months. Sage and I had been out late at the library studying, and when we went to get in her car, he pounced out of nowhere, begging me for another chance. Sage scrambled to unlock the doors, and when I bolted in the passenger side, he held the door open with one hand and had a knife in the other. He said he'd cut my face up and kill her if I didn't let him in the car. At the time, I didn't know what else to do or how to defend myself."

"That's why you know how to shoot a gun."

She nods and continues. "He had Sage drive to a seedy part of town and park behind an old rundown building. When he kicked the door open, Sage stuffed her phone in the back of her jeans. He led us up a set of old rusted-out stairs. I was terrified he was going to kill us, and I knew I had to do something. He shoved us inside a moldy-smelling apartment and locked the door behind him. I pleaded with him not to kill us and told him I'd do whatever he wanted, knowing if I could get him away from Sage, she'd call for help."

Everything in me wants to get up and punch a wall. I refrain. "Did he touch you?"

Tears roll down her cheeks. "I went into the bedroom with him, and he tore off my shirt. I can still feel his stubble against my neck and the stench of alcohol on his breath. I distracted him when I told him that things between us would be different. That I'd drop the restraining order, and I convinced him that I'd run off with him. It was just long enough for the police to arrive."

"Thank God for Sage."

"To say he was furious is mild."

"Did he go to jail?"

"He served six years. Turns out he'd had a prior arrest but no conviction for stalking another young woman."

"Has he contacted you since?"

"I received a letter from him, but the police were unable to track it down. I saw him in the grocery store watching me. That's when I let Sage convince me to pack up everything and move here."

"Are you sure he doesn't know where you are?"

"My dad helped me leave in the middle of the night and had several of his military buddies follow me just to be sure."

I move to face her and wipe her tears with the back of my hand. "I'm so sorry any of that happened to you." She moves into my arms, and I hold her until she drifts off to sleep. Reaching across her, I cover her with a pale pink knitted blanket that's been stitched back together several times and recall her telling me about her mother making it for her and how much she must miss her.

When I hear the front door open, I slip out of bed so as not to wake her and tiptoe out of the room, leaving the door cracked.

Sage is putting her purse down when she sees me. "Everything alright?"

I walk over and hug her. "She told me what happened and that you saved her."

"Wow, she actually talked about that day?" She leans back to look me in the eye.

"Every detail, and if I ever get my hands on the bastard, he'll never touch another woman again." I exhale sharply and run my hand over my face. "My fear is that if he's determined to find her, he will."

"You think her stalker would be crazy enough to follow her to Montana?"

"I do, and I'm sure it's in the back of her mind."

"She blames herself for ever having anything to do with him."

"It's not her fault he's a sick bastard."

"She avoided any type of romantic relationship since him...until you."

Meandering to the couch, I sit. "It's no wonder you disliked me so much, but I want you to know I'd never hurt her. I have my own demons with women, but there's something about her that feels so different."

She plops beside me. "Perhaps your demons like one another," she snorts.

"I'm going to have Chase do some digging on the whereabouts of this clown." I hand her my phone.

"Give me his name and his last known whereabouts."

She adjusts to face me. "I was wrong about you. You're a good guy."

"You judged me on what I showed you and everyone else in this town, and I'm going to change their perception of me. I've made a lot of mistakes, and I'm willing to own up to them."

She covers my hand with hers. "I'm rooting for the two of you. She needs a protective cowboy in her life."

10

THAYER

Stretching, I feel the sunrise on my face looming through the cracks in the blinds. "Blaise," I whisper his name, recalling falling asleep in the warmth of his arms. "I was fooling myself thinking I was any different than any other woman to him. The sun rising must be his call to do the walk of shame." My heart feels heavy because I really do like him.

Crawling to the side of the bed, I make a halfhearted attempt to brush out the wrinkles in my pink top but don't bother changing before meandering into the kitchen to perk a pot of coffee. My bare feet stick to the ground when I see Blaise's long frame sprawled out on the two-seater couch, sound asleep with his

Stetson lying on the floor. "He didn't leave," I say quietly.

Walking quietly, I pick up his hat and set it on the coffee table, then peek out the front door. Sage's car is not in the driveway. She often disappears early in the morning to take photos. She calls it her church time when nothing else is around to disturb the critters she wants to capture behind the lens.

Crouching, I take in the handsome man that was so sweet last night. I want to trust him and fall head over heels in love with him. Dabbing my lips together, I gently place a kiss on his chin.

Dark lashes flutter against his cheek, and his green eyes darken as soon as he sees me. "Mornin'," he grunts.

"You stayed." I whisk hair off his forehead.

"You're playing with fire touching me," he rasps and lifts his head, looking at his tenting jeans.

"Maybe I want to get burned," I divulge, a little unsure of myself, and my fingers fumble unbuttoning his collar.

He catches my arm by the wrist. "If you're not sure, don't start something that I won't be able to stop."

He lets go, and I continue to unfasten his shirt, pushing it out of the way and appreciating the ripple of his muscles the action brings to his skin. Smiling, I slowly press my lips to the middle of his sternum, and I hear him hiss. An unfamiliar building between my legs taunts me to continue, bravely moving my lips further down and sucking his nipple into my mouth. His fists are at his sides, keeping himself from touching me, allowing me the freedom to explore his vexing body.

The moment my hands meet his belt buckle, they shake. He sits up, placing me between his legs, and we're eye to eye. He grazes my jawline with a kiss, and my entire body hums in delight.

"I want you so damn badly." His breath blows across my skin. With a steady hand, he flicks my small white button open as if it were not even there to hold my blouse closed.

"You're so beautiful," his voice is loaded with raw appreciation. His hand touches my flesh as he pushes the shirt from my shoulders, leaving me in my pink bra. His wide grin covers his face. "I knew it was pink." Then he kisses me until my lips are swollen, not missing even a crevice to taste me.

My desire for him is so out of control I want to rip his clothes off and straddle him for hours. He moans when I move to his buckle again, and I swear my brain is going to short-circuit if I can't get my wanting hands on him fast enough.

He moves in, unzipping his jeans and giving me access. His cock is so hard I feel like he'll explode at any minute, but I love the feel of him cupped in my hand.

"If you stroke me, it will be over," he growls, standing, taking me with him. Reaching behind me, he unclasps my bra, but before he lets it fall off of me, he hesitates. "Are you sure this is what you want?"

"Yes," I say unequivocally with a nod.

Sweeping me off my feet, he carries me to the bedroom and closes the door using his foot before he sets me on mine, then he rips the bra off and tosses it on the floor. "I want to see you," he says, taking a step back.

I boldly wiggle out of my pants, taking my panties with it, and I'm stark naked in front of him and feel no shame. The way he's looking at me makes me feel sexy, and I want his eyes on every inch of me.

He rips his jeans off, and I swallow hard, seeing this beautiful man in all his glory. I press my thighs together, and his eyes track to my core.

"I want you to spread those for me so I can lose myself in you. My cock is aching to be buried deep inside of you," he says, and my need for him grows.

He bends down, picks up his jeans and pulls a condom from his wallet, and rolls it down his length. Wasting no more words, his hands are all over me as he lays me on my back, crawling above me, kissing me, sucking at my tongue, my lips, one nipple, then the other like he's tasting my lust for him while pledging so much more and me thirsting for his unspoken promise.

Parting my legs, I wrap them around him as my fingers tangle in his hair.

A sheen of sweat covers his body, and he stills. "I'm fighting like hell not to thrust inside of you like a wild animal." When he moves again, his cock rubs against the slickness of my clit, and I moan, arching my back and pressing into him, wanting more pressure.

I skim my hands down his back and dig my nails into his ass. "That feels so good," I hum.

His mouth worships every curve, every freckle, every inch of my body. What started as me being brazen has left me at his mercy to do whatever he wants with me, and I have every intention of letting him.

He reaches between us, placing the tip of his cock at my entrance. "The beast in me wants to fuck you." He pushes in an inch and then backs off. "But I want to take my time and love you." His eyes are half-lidded, and I can tell he's struggling with which side of him will win control or lose.

I answer him, laying my fingers on his lip. "I want the wild side of you." My voice is breathy.

Shifting his hips, he fills me completely, and I gasp. In that one savage thrust, he claims me deeper than I've ever felt. Pulling out, he spreads my legs wider and repositions himself, then painstakingly slow, he sinks into my heat, and I clamp down around him with a sound of despair leaving my chest. I curve my legs tighter, pushing him deeper, feeling him everywhere.

"Surrender to me," he says in a way that I know he's feeling the same frenzied need for release. He thrusts harder and harder, and his warm tongue swarms my nipple to a painful peak, calling for my orgasm to yield to his command of surrender.

With no control, I cry out his name over and over as my body tenses around his deep penetration. In the midst of it, I pull his lips to mine with a newfound hunger while waves ripple through my sex. I can feel his muscles flex, and his movements become rougher until I climax again. This time, we ride our orgasms out together with our teeth clashing against each other's skin like untamed animals. Just when I think he's finished and I can't come anymore, he leans back and lifts my leg and pushes my thigh against my breasts, and moves deeper than before, causing one more tidal wave of pleasure for both of us.

I haven't recovered from my breathlessness when there's a rap on my door. "Please tell me you're locked in there with Blaise and not some madman," Sage hollers.

I go to speak, but Blaise's palm covers my mouth. "You don't ever have to worry about anything happening to her again," he speaks loud enough for her to hear him.

"Good, now maybe I can stop listening to the vibrator turn on at night."

I want to die from embarrassment, and I just might kill her myself.

Blaise kisses me, and I hear the sound of a drawer being opened. Rising, he's holding my vibrator. "Not that you'll need it, but we could have some fun with this." He waggles his brows and then turns it on, and I squeal when he touches my already tender clit with his tongue, taking what he wants before the vibrator glides between my thighs. Any and all coherent thoughts are lost in him.

11

BLAISE

"We really should get out of bed," Thayer hums with her lips pressed to the middle of my bare chest.

My head spins at the fact that I'm still in her arms. There was no fight-or-flight moment for me with her but awkwardness in staying present. This is very unfamiliar territory, yet it feels so right. "I'm not ready to leave your side." I pout and pat her on the ass.

"I seriously have work to do, and I need to drop off a few signed paperbacks at the local bookstore that I promised the owner."

"I can do that on my way home if you'd like."

She sits and covers her breasts with the sheet. "I have a better idea. How about if you come with me, and we can grab some goodies at the bakery?"

"Good plan." As I reach for my jeans, my cell phone rings. "What's up, River?" He proceeds to tell me the hay baler broke down, and they can't get it running. "I'll be there as quick as I can," I tell him, drawing my pants up over my hips.

"You can't go with me?" Thayer pokes out her bottom lip, and I find it enticing, swooping in for a kiss.

"We're still going, just moving a little faster. Now get that gorgeous ass out of bed before I lose my job calling off for a sex day."

Shuffling to her feet, she runs into the bathroom and yells loud enough for me to hear her while I put my boots on. "Have you done that before?"

"Done what?"

"Called off for a day of sex?"

Chuckling, I stomp to the door and poke my head inside. "I've never had a full day of sex."

Her cute nose scrunches. "Sorry, I shouldn't have asked you that. I momentarily forgot you're more the wham-bam-thank you-ma'am kinda guy."

"Ouch." I laugh.

She pulls her hair into a ponytail and swings her hips in my direction. "Thank you for not leaving last night."

"I'm right where I want to be." She stands on her tiptoes and kisses me.

"My body is sore from the best sex I've ever had. I don't care, nor do I want to know how you've possessed such skills as long as they're only used on me from now on."

"I can't promise you I'm not going to screw up, but I can assure you they'll be no one else in my bed."

"Fair enough. Now get your ass moving before I have to call your employer myself and explain why you'll be a no-show today."

I hand her my phone, and she grins. "Don't threaten me with a good time, and expect me to balk at it."

She howls and pushes the phone away. "Alright, cowboy, let's get out of here." I follow her into the living room.

"It's about time you two came up for air. Not saying I'm jealous or anything," Sage says before biting into a slice of pizza.

I snatch a piece from her plate.

"Hey!"

"I need to replenish my energy," I tease and wink.

Thayer piles in her car, and I take my truck into town, parking close to the bakery and calling in my takeout order.

The Daily Dose of Reading is a mom-and-pop store. In a corner nook, there's a lone reader sitting on the floor with a child in her lap, dramatically reading to him. It reminds me of all the times my mom forced me to go to the library, hoping she'd get me to fall in love with books. She'd read everything she could get her hands on, introducing me to my favorite childhood book, *Ferdinand the Bull*.

I find the romance area and walk up and down the aisle until I locate a section dedicated to Thayer

Hawkins on an end display cap. Flipping one of the books over, I read the blurb, then tuck it under my arm and make my way to the check-out counter. Once I purchase it, I nestle into a cozy seat calling my name. With my head in the book, I scan a few pages and then hear a throat clearing.

"What are you doing?"

"Rumor has it, there's this fantastic author I need to read." I wave the book in the air.

She holds her hand out, laughing. "Come on."

"Are you done already?"

"Yes, and I'm starving. Someone caused me to miss not only breakfast but lunch too."

I get to my feet and follow her to the street. "Are you complaining?"

"Not at all," she snorts. "You've inspired me."

I snatch her hand. "Wait, you're not putting what we did in a book, are you?"

She takes the paperback out of my hand. "Read chapter seventeen if you want some inspiration of your own."

I know we had sex for hours, but my cock has found new life. As we walk, I locate the chapter.

"You might want to read it when you're not in public. It might have a certain effect on you." Her gaze narrows in on my crotch.

I slam the book shut between both of my hands. "Good idea. You've already gotten me all worked up."

Her face turns pink as she swings open the glass door to the bakery, and the most heavenly scent of cinnamon slaps me in the face.

"How are the honeymooners?" Lisa, Kat's partner, asks as she's boxing up baked goods behind the counter.

"I'm sure they aren't thinking about us one little bit." I chuckle, and she hands me the box. "Thanks for getting these ready for me."

"You aren't staying?" Thayer angles her head up to look at me.

"Sorry. I really need to get to the ranch." I pay for my goods and toss cash on the counter. "Get her whatever she wants." I turn to face Thayer. "Take something home to Sage, and make sure to tell her it's from me."

"You're such a suck-up," she hoots.

"I'll call you later." Kissing her softly, I notice a slight frown form between her brows. "I will call you later." I repeat each word slowly, staring into her eyes so she knows I mean business.

"Okay," she says in a hush.

Tossing the box on the passenger's seat, I head to the ranch, and the smell of cinnamon follows me through the house. Granger and Miller nearly snatch the lid off the box opening it.

"These are my favorite." The white icing drips down Granger's chin.

"They're my mom's secret recipe." Miller smiles with pride before he sticks half of the roll into his mouth.

River stomps his boots off before he swings open the screen door. Black grease mars his hands with a smudge on his chin. "I attempted to fix that da...dang hay baler," he chooses his words carefully. I heard Greer getting on him for swearing around the boys.

Granger repeated a few choice words and found himself in a world of trouble, along with his father.

"I'll get right on it."

The boys hustle out with another roll. "You didn't come home last night." River turns the water on in the sink and scrubs his hands.

"Thayer was a bit out of sorts, and I didn't want to leave her alone."

He towel dries his hands and leans his hip on the counter. "That has to be a first for you."

"She's got me all tied up in knots. From the moment I laid eyes on her, I wanted more. I don't know what the hell is wrong with me."

"Why do you assume there's something wrong with what you're feeling?"

"Honestly, it scares the shit out of me the depth of what I feel for her so quickly."

"I get that, but I think the heart knows what it wants when you meet the right person."

"What if that's not it? Perhaps I'm just caught up in the notion of love with all of you getting married and moving on with your lives."

He throws the towel down and places the palms of his hands on the breakfast bar. "Let me ask you something. In all these years since Rachel died, have you ever had any inkling of a connection with a woman? I'm not talking about sex."

I close my eyes and blow out a long, exaggerated breath. "I'm ashamed to say no. It was all meaning-less. It wasn't that I didn't want to feel something. I just didn't."

He stands tall and chuckles. "I don't believe that suddenly with all of us finding love, would trigger that kind of emotion. You might want to explore it more with this woman." He slaps the counter.

"I'm scared." I swallow my admission hard.

"Of what?"

"She's going to break me."

He steps closer. "Then you have to decide if she's worth the risk or not."

His words mull around in my head, fogging up my thoughts. "I've wasted enough time. I'll get to work on the hay baler." My boots scuff the floor on my way to the screen door.

"I find it ironic that you can repair any engine known to man, but that thing inside your chest stays broken."

"Yeah, too bad I can't just order new parts for it." I laugh and push through the door.

As I dig deep into the engine, my mind flashes back to the day I found Rachel hanging with a rope around her neck from a beam in her family's barn. I've never been able to erase the vision of her purple lips and how cold she was down to her blue nails. Anger that lives deep inside of me boils up, and I launch a wrench through the air. It bounces off the wall, crashing to the floor with a loud echo. "Damn it, Rachel," I yell at the top of my lungs. "Why? Why didn't you ask for help?" I exhale a jagged breath, and tears loom in the corner of my eyes with a familiar heaviness seizing my chest. I can't do this. I won't put Thayer through the agony I can't control. I'll end it before it gets out of hand.

Digging my phone from my back pocket, I search for

her number, and my finger lingers over her name. Clenching my teeth, I toss it in the toolbox and open one of the small red drawers I stashed a bottle of pills in when I decided I wasn't going to take them anymore. Popping open the cap, one falls into my palm, and I glare at it as if it's the devil. Another rolls out, and I swallow both of them, choking them down with no water.

Delving back into the engine, I try to keep my mind off Thayer, but my fingertips burn with the memory of touching every part of her. And as quick as that flashback fills my mind, Rachel steals it. It's a battle back and forth for the rest of the day. It's dark out before I realize the day is gone and nighttime has settled in, and I surrender to the day.

Knox is loading the fridge with leftovers when I walk through the back door into the kitchen. Slipping my phone out of my pocket, I turn it off.

"You look like crap. Did you get the hay baler fixed?"

"No, but I did figure out what's wrong with it, and I'll have to go into town tomorrow to get the part."

"Are you hungry?"

"I'm starved. I haven't eaten all day."

"Mercy cooked up a batch of fried chicken and biscuits. I'll warm you a plate."

"I can do it myself. I'm sure you'd like to get home to Hardin."

"I don't mind. Besides, you look like you could use some company." She places the dish in the microwave and programs in the time. "Old ghosts running around in that head of yours?" she asks when she faces me.

"Obviously, I've lost my talent for hiding my emotions, and I'm wearing them on my sleeves." I chuckle.

"Is there anything I can do to help?"

"No. I just want to fill my belly and get a long hot shower." A pang of guilt hits me, knowing I promised Thayer I'd call her.

The microwave pings, and she takes out the plate, setting it in front of me. "You know, I love the fun-loving, wild side of you. This sadness I see in your eyes makes me uneasy."

"I haven't learned to master the wild side with my demons."

"They should learn to play together. Don't lose that wildness, and if you'll tame the voice of your demons and take the lessons you've learned, you'll be one hell of a man." She slaps me on the back as she heads out.

Scarfing down my food, I lick my fingers and then stick my plate in the dishwasher before bounding up the stairs straight into a hot shower, scrubbing as much of the grease from my hands as I can.

Drying off, I wrap the towel around my waist and stare into the foggy mirror, not wanting to see the full image of the man glaring back at me. I've not been able to look him in the eye for a long time, afraid of what I'll see. "I'm sorry, Thayer. It has to be over before it really begins," I utter and turn off the light, tossing the towel on the floor and crawling into bed only to find no sleep.

12

THAYER

"I'll be back next week. I'm so excited about this photo shoot in Arizona, and the warmth on my skin won't hurt either." Sage is packing the last of her clothes in a suitcase.

"You're going to do amazing." I'm thrilled for her, but I'm having a hard time mustering any enthusiasm.

"What's got your face all scrunched up this morning?"

"Nothing. Don't worry about me." I wave her off and plaster on a fake smile. "I've got loads of work to do to meet my deadline."

"Does that mean you won't be hanging out with the hottie?" She tosses her backpack over her shoulder.

Groaning on the inside, I don't want to tell her that Blaise broke his promise. Besides, he probably just got busy and figured it was too late to call me. "I'm going to lock myself in my cave and only come out to eat." My fingers are crossed behind my back. I don't want to spill the beans on the surprise I'm working on for her.

"Alright. I'll see you in a week." She hugs me.

"Are you sure I can't drive you to the airport?"

She glances at her watch. "My Uber driver should be pulling up any minute." As if on cue, a horn blows. "That would be it."

"Text me photos," I holler as she bolts out of the door.

I spend a few minutes on the phone with my father, assuring him that I'm doing okay. When I moved here, I made sure my address was linked to a post office box in Boston and my dad ships mail in Sage's name to a PO Box in town. He's done everything he can to protect me, and I love him for it.

Lisa set up a time for me to meet her at the building she and Katherine own in town to check out a space for Sage's gallery. She texted me that the bakery was busy and she was running late, but to please wait for her. There's a bench outside of the building facing Main Street. I love to people watch, so I cop a squat and adjust my sunglasses to cut down on the mid-morning glare and inhale the fresh, clean air smells while periodically checking my phone for a text message or missed call from Blaise. There's nothing. I'm tempted to call him. Instead, I shove my phone in my purse.

I try in vain to focus on a plot twist in the book I'm writing and take notes on my phone, but I can't get my mind off Blaise. More specifically, how my body reacted to his touch.

His words in my ear.

His tongue on my clit.

The sound he made when he let go.

I whip my head around when a horn blows, followed by a few curse words. I get to my feet when I see Blaise crossing the narrow street between cars. Starting after him, I stop when he opens a car door parked along the curb for a strikingly beautiful woman dressed in a white blouse and navy slacks.

She gets out and smiles at him, and he ushers her into the brewery where I met him. "It's probably nothing. A cousin. A friend." I shrug but can't stop my feet from moving to the crosswalk until I hear Lisa call my name.

"Thayer! I'm so sorry I'm late. Thank you for waiting for me." Her keys rattle, unlocking the door.

I bite my upper lip looking across the street, then back at Lisa. "It was no problem." I change directions and follow her lead. "Wow, this place is great. I love all the modern architecture."

Crisp white walls surround me, and pine wood floors stretch the entire length of the building, with matching wood on the stairs and handrails. Rooms are divided with glass walls and black polished finishings.

"We have office spaces available in all sizes for up to twelve people. There's a conference room on each floor and private booths to make phone calls. The cost I quoted you includes everything, and I picked out the perfect spot for a gallery." She stops in front of an office that has two glass walls, a solid wall, and a large window that faces Main Street.

Setting my purse on the ground, I take in the space. "I love the high ceilings and the feel of openness in the small space. We can install some strategic lighting on the back wall to display her artwork and could build a free-standing wall so she can use both sides."

"That's a great idea."

I spin in a circle, checking it out. "Some modern shelving could go there"—I point—"and easels facing the glass walls to draw people into the gallery."

"You said this space isn't for you?"

"It's for my best friend. She's an amazing photographer, and she's talked about opening a gallery for years but keeps making every excuse in the world as to why she can't. I'm taking the rationales away and renting this space for her."

"Wow. What a great gift for her."

"She's worth it, and she's done so much for me. Where do I sign?"

"I'll email everything over to you, and you can sign it electronically and send it back to me."

"Are all these other spaces rented?"

"Our opening isn't until next week, and we're already at seventy-five percent capacity. There will be a hair salon catty-corner to this one. A real estate office is going upstairs. We have a web designer and a marketer also, along with several other small businesses. Katherine has a kitchen with workstations in the very back."

"You ladies have done a remarkable job. I can't wait to surprise Sage."

"You're welcome to start setting up anytime you'd like. Once you've signed the lease, stop by the bakery, and I'll give you a key you swipe to unlock the doors. Or Katherine is due back this week, so you can get one from her. Either way. If you'll give me some dimensions, I can work on the floating wall and have it ready for you by opening day."

"Great. I'll shop for some shelving and have it delivered." I pick up my purse.

"I look forward to doing business with you, and I could use some updated artwork in my bakery."

"Thanks, Lisa," I say as we part ways.

My car key is gripped in my hand, but I can't make myself unlock it. I take off toward the crosswalk leading to the brewery. A nervous heat prickles underneath my skin. It's a mixture of fear and anger, wanting to know who Blaise is having lunch with.

"How many in your party?" the hostess greets me.

"I'm looking for someone," I say, peering around her. A couple slips in behind me, and I walk into the bar area and see Blaise nestled in a corner booth with the woman sitting across from him. His head is slumped, his hands propped on his cheeks. The woman reaches over and takes his hand, and smiles. I can't hear what's being said, but I see him react to her, and it tears at my gut.

"You couldn't even make it a day without seeing someone else. I'm such an idiot," I hiss under my breath and stride out before he sees me.

Swatting away my tears, I sit in my car, grasping the steering wheel. "You barely know a guy, who you've been warned is a player, and you're upset why?" I ask myself. "Why did I think I'd be any different than any other woman he's taken to bed. I deserve it. My choices in men really suck." I sniff hard and pull out onto the single-lane traffic of Main Street. Boston was so busy compared to the quietness of this town, and I came here to feel safe again, not go to get my heart broken by another man. I let my guard down for a hot minute going from one man who became completely obsessed with me to another who only wanted in my skirt.

The light turns yellow, then red, forcing me to tap my brakes. A man in a ball cap and khakis steps into the crosswalk, and my insides shudder. "It can't be him." He continues to walk with his head lowered until he reaches the other side, and I crane my neck to try to get a good look at his face.

The car behind taps its horn when the light turns green and I don't move. The man wearing the hat turns to the noise and I exhale in relief that it's not him.

"Get it together, girl. Now, you're imagining things." I wave an apology to the person behind me and ease through the light arriving home in no time.

It seems strange knowing Sage isn't here, and with what I just thought I saw, it makes me uneasy. Locking the deadbolt, I toss my purse on the back of the couch and snag a bottle of water from the fridge, and head straight for my room, locking myself inside. Adjusting the height of my chair, I open my laptop and stare blankly at the screen, trying to recall the notes I had made. Instead, all I can think about is Blaise. Despite my disappointment, my body feels the attraction that hummed between us every time I was close to him. The way he kissed me was awfully convincing that he felt the same thing. When his chest crashed against mine, I wanted him more than I wanted to breathe. The romance writer in me wanted the bad boy to change for her.

Rolling my shoulders, I sit tall. "That only happens in fiction, not real life." I tap open my manuscript, and I pile on every emotion I'm feeling into the words, making my alpha male an asshole, only to go back and delete an entire chapter. "You're not going to be a complete dick." I chomp on my lower lip and jump when I hear a banging on the front door.

Unlocking my bedroom door, I stand in the hallway and listen.

"Thayer! It's me, Blaise." He pounds harder on the door.

"Go away!" I yell, barreling through the living room.

"Please let me in. I'm sorry I didn't call you last night."

"You have a lot more than that to be sorry for! I saw you having lunch with one of your floozies!"

"It's not what you think."

"Oh really." I plant my arms over my chest and tap my toe on the floor. "Who was she?"

He's silent.

"Are you still there?" I press my ear to the door.

"Yes." His response lost all vigor.

"Are you going to tell me who she is?"

13

BLAISE

H ours earlier...

"Have you been in the garage all night?" River asks, toting two cups of coffee.

Tugging the bandanna from my back pocket, I wipe my hands, and he holds out a mug. "Couldn't sleep, so I thought I'd get a jump on cleaning up these parts before I put it back together. I'll run into town this morning and get what I need and have this thing running by the end of the day."

"Do you want to talk about what's eating you?"

"No," I answer quickly, keeping my gaze on the concrete floor.

"You know where to find me if you change your mind," he says and saunters out.

I lean on the hay baler and sip my coffee. Telling myself that I'm no good for Thayer hasn't settled well, my heart has been racing all night long, and my head has gone to a dark place. I'm meant to be alone for the rest of my life. Sharing this part of me will only hurt her.

"Damn it!" I yell, and my hot coffee sloshes over the sides and down my arm. "Shit! Shit! Shit!" I toss the cup and use the bandana to wipe it off. "This woman has to be tied in knots," I grit out. "I don't know what the hell to do."

Picking my phone up from the toolbox, I ache to call her. Instead, I call the other woman in my life that helps things make sense.

"Dr. Shields," I say as soon as she answers. "Do you have any openings in your schedule today?"

"Not in the office, no."

"You said if I needed to talk, you'd fit me in. I have to be in town this morning to pick up a part. Is there any way you could meet me?"

"Let me check my schedule. Hold on a second."

I wait while she looks.

"I have a small window of time at eleven."

"Great. Meet me at the brewery."

"I'll be there, but I won't have long."

"I understand. See you soon."

I run inside and change clothes, avoiding making eye contact with anyone so they don't try to draw me into a deep conversation. I know they only do it out of love, but I don't want them drawn into my misery.

Parking in the auto parts store lot, once I've made my purchase, I decide to leave my truck there and walk the two blocks to the brewery. When I see Dr. Shields parking, without thinking, I dart between cars and nearly get hit by one. The horn blowing and profanity have me hustling to get to the other side.

"Hey," I say, opening her door.

"You must be really distracted." She points to where I crossed the road.

I expel the air from my lungs. "My head's not in the right place."

"Thus, why you called me," she says, pushing the lock button on her remote.

The brewery has just opened, so we get the pick of the place. I find a booth in the bar area near the back. She slides in one side, and I, the other.

"What's going on?" She jumps right in.

"I told you about the woman I met."

"Yes."

"I slept with her...I mean..." My words trail off, and I hang my head.

"And you left her bed empty."

"No. I stayed the night and the next day. It was amazing."

"That's a good thing, Blaise. So what's the issue?"

"Before I left, I told her I'd call her, and then somewhere in there, I danced with the devil in my head and convinced myself I wasn't any good for her."

"You didn't call her."

I nod. "The problem is, I really want to be with her, but I don't know how." I rest my face in my hands.

My eyes lift toward hers when she touches my hand. "Admitting that is a milestone for you."

"But what if I'm not capable of true intimacy with any woman?"

"That's a natural feeling after what you've been through. Suicide of a loved one is a difficult path to maneuver. It took multiple sessions for you to tell me what happened. I think you need to practice sharing your feelings openly. It's part of the healing process. When that voice in your head tells you you're not good enough, or you somehow blame yourself for Rachel's choice, and that deep depression sets in, tell it all to go to hell. You are good enough, and you can't hold yourself accountable for what she did. It's time to let go, and I think this woman may be the perfect person to help you with that."

"She probably thinks I've already tucked tail and moved on and did nothing but use her."

"You're a smart man. I think you can figure out how to get her to change her mind."

I sit back, letting my head fall against the booth. "I don't know. Perhaps I should give it a few months and see how things go."

"Don't do that again," she snaps.

"Do what?"

"Put an end date on it. Take one day at a time, and sometimes when you feel that panic hitting you, minute by minute might be better. Let your heart guide you, not that messed up head of yours." She glances at her watch. "I'm sorry, but I really can't stay much longer. I can pencil you in for tomorrow. In the meantime, go to her and tell her your story."

"Can I buy you lunch and have it sent to your office?"

"I love the black and blue salad." She smiles and scoots out of the booth.

"Thanks for meeting me. I really appreciate it."

"You're welcome, and we're going to get you through this. Just please take the meds I prescribed you for now."

She hustles out the door, and I order a burger and a salad for her that I'll drop off on my way home.

Starting my truck, I have every intention of going back to the ranch to put on the new part for the hay baler, but as I get to the edge of town, I do a U-turn and direct my path to Thayer's place.

My chest squeezes the moment I see her car parked out front, and my temples throb. Yanking down the visor, I look into the eyes of the man I hide from.

"I want this."

"I want this woman."

"I want more."

Flipping it in position, I storm out of my truck like a man with a sole mission in mind. My fist stops short of knocking on the door, and I do an about-face three times before I rap my knuckles on the wood.

"Thayer! It's me, Blaise." Taking a step back, I wait for her to answer me.

"Go away!" she yells, and I can hear heavy footsteps.

"Please let me in. I'm sorry I didn't call you last night."

"You have a lot more than that to be sorry for! I saw you having lunch with one of your floozies!"

How? Where was she? "It's not what you think."

"Oh really." She pauses for a second. "Who was she?"

I grind my teeth into my bottom lip. How am I going to explain it to her? I don't want to tell her all the gory details of my past.

"Are you still there?" Her voice is softer.

"Yes," I respond, but my tone has lost all its vigor, and I fight the sadness stealing my bravery.

"Are you going to tell me who she is?"

"Please let me in," I beg, pressing my forehead to the door until I hear her unlock it. Stepping back further, believing she'll invite me inside. Instead, she faces me on the porch.

"I'm waiting."

"I know I owe you an explanation about why I didn't call."

"Among other things." Her fingernails clutch into her hip. "The truth is you not calling wasn't any big deal. I assumed you got busy, and it was too late to call. I don't own your life, Blaise. Hell, we've barely just met. This whole thing with us got out of hand so quickly, and honestly, I have no right to ask you who she was. I knew your reputation, and it was my choice to take a chance. I lost."

"But you didn't." I ease toward her, and she inches back. "I want more with you than I've ever thought possible. You make me feel things that have been lost inside of me for years. I tend to shut things down and bury them."

Her eyes narrow, but not with anger. "Why are you lost, Blaise? Tell me."

I clutch my chest. "I really need something to drink." That panic Evie spoke of thuds in my veins, consuming me.

"Come inside, and I'll get you some water."

I follow her into the kitchen and grip the sink with both hands and close my eyes to keep the room from spinning.

"Hey," she says, gently touching my shoulder. "Drink this."

My hand shakes, unscrewing the cap. Gulping it down, it spills down my chin, and I wipe it off with the tail of my shirt.

"You really are a mess, aren't you?" The tenderness in the crevices of her eyes calms me a bit. "Come sit on the couch with me."

"Where's Sage?" I ask, not wanting her to hear me spill my guts.

"She's out of town until next week. It's just the two of us." Taking my hand, she walks me into the living room, and I sit, laying my hat on the coffee table. I lean against the back, and she sits with her legs folded beneath her, facing me.

"You can trust me," she says, laying her fingertips on my thigh.

Taking in a deep breath, I dive in. "I banished the types of feelings I have for you years ago, swearing

I'd never let them surface for another woman. You're blatantly aware that I've had many lovers but no real connections...until you. As long as my relationships stayed superficial, all was good. But, as soon as any of the women started showing deeper feelings, it was my cue that it was over. I go into every relationship with an expiration date, and I have every excuse ready to end it." I glance into her eyes, and they have tears spilling out.

"Who hurt you so badly?"

I leap off the couch and pace around the table, periodically running my hands through my hair. A long silence stretches between us before I speak. "Rachel was my high school sweetheart. She was the prom queen, and I was the quarterback. Sounds like something out of a Hallmark movie. Anyway, I thought she and I would live happily ever after. Grow old together, have six or seven babies, and live a good life."

"What happened?"

"You think you really know someone, but you don't. Some scars are so deeply hidden that no one sees them. I never saw it coming."

"She ended things with you and broke your heart?"

I shove my hands in my pockets and lick my lips. "She committed suicide and I found her hanging in her parents' barn."

She gasps, covering her mouth. "No."

"She left a note saying how much she battled depression and no amount of therapy or drugs were helping. Her soul was tormented, and she couldn't find release from it other than death, and I had no fucking idea." My jaw rocks back and forth, trying to hold it together. "I blamed myself for not seeing it, but I was so damn angry at her for leaving me the way she did."

"That explains the expiration date you set in your mind with women. You don't want to be left."

"Bingo." I tap my nose.

She meets me on her feet and wraps her arms around my waist. "I'm so sorry."

"I blamed myself for years, but I finally understood how she hid her pain. I've gotten really good at putting on a mask when I feel I'm being towed underwater. I found myself withdrawing, putting distance between me and everyone I loved, including my family. They doubled down, and I found my connection with them again."

"I know that feeling of guilt, not in the same manner as you, but feeling helpless over someone else's choice. In the back of my mind, I did something to cause my stalker Brent's obsession with me. Until you...I haven't been intimately involved with another man because of it."

"And I go and screw us up." I kiss the top of her head.

"Who was the woman at the brewery?"

"My therapist. When I left here yesterday, I got lost in the chaos of my own thoughts and sunk into a depression, convincing myself I wasn't good enough for you and it wouldn't take you long to figure it out, and you'd run. So I set an end date before we even began, but this time it was so that it wouldn't hurt so bad, not because I wanted to bolt. The power of rejection rocked me to the core."

"I feel awful that I jumped to a conclusion about her."

"Don't. What else were you supposed to think, given my reputation."

She steps out of my arms. "What makes me different than the others?"

"Honestly, I don't know, but there's some magnetism between us like I've never felt, and I'm lost at how to handle it."

"I know exactly how to manage it."

14

THAYER

Meshing my fingers with his, I lead him to my bedroom, step on my tiptoes, and gently kiss his lips, wanting to ease his pain, if only for a moment in time. I keep it slow, wanting to savor him.

"Thayer," he murmurs between laps of our tongues.

Goose bumps ripple over my skin, and I pull him closer, needing to give him my warmth and comfort, banishing the painful memories that pull him into darkness, giving him my light, my love.

"Thayer," he whispers again, then clasps my hips with his hands. "As much as I want this, I can't."

I draw back to look into his eyes.

"I mean, physically, I can." He peers down between us at the bulge in his jeans. "If I want more with you, I have to change how I've always done things to tear down the walls I've built to protect myself."

"Are you saying sex is off the table?" I raise a disappointed brow.

"For now, yes. Our relationship can't be based purely on sex. I want to get to know you and fall in love with no end date in mind."

"That's what I want, too, but my body heats up every time I'm near you."

"Trust me, I feel the same way, and I'm not saying in ten minutes I won't let my other head win out, but I'd like to try."

His honesty tugs at my heart, and I move from his grasp. "Alright, then my body is off-limits until you trust what's growing between us."

He grins, and I know exactly what he's thinking.

"Not body parts growing between us." I point at his crotch and laugh.

He clears his throat. "Thanks for clarifying that."

"I'm willing to give you what you want, but just know I'll need to up my stock of batteries," I snort, "and it's all your fault. Since sex is off the table, what do you suggest we do?"

"You said you like to shoot. How about after I finish work today, I take you to one of the ranges in the mountains?"

"I'd like that. I'll pack us a picnic to take along."

He starts walking backward.

"Where are you going?"

"First, to take a cold shower, then to work. I'll call you when I'm on my way to pick you up."

"Are you sure you're going to call this time?"

"I'm not going to promise you anything. I'll show you." He skips out with his heart much lighter than when he arrived. His story is awful. I can't imagine being in his shoes, finding the person I loved hanging lifeless from the end of a noose. She ended her misery but thrust him into a world of heartache. It explains a lot, that's for sure.

Blaise wanting to break his habit of jumping into meaningless sex with women is a good start. It's going to leave me horny as heck every time I'm around him, but in the end, I hope he's worth it.

I scatter to my phone when it rings in the other room.

"Hey, it's your roomie. I wanted to let you know that I've arrived safely."

"That's great," I exhale.

"You sound disappointed," she snickers.

"No, no, not at all. I'm distracted. Blaise just left."

"Oh, so you're coming down from a glorious orgasm," she howls into the phone.

"Actually, quite the opposite. He's sworn off sex."

"You broke him?" She can't hide her merriment.

"He wants things to be different with us."

"Not having sex would definitely be a change of pace for a guy like him."

"I think it's sweet."

"I gotta run. I'll call you tomorrow."

"Have fun, and you're going to be great."

"Thanks."

I hang up and return to my laptop, only for my phone to ring again. I answer it without looking, thinking it's Sage. "Did you call back to razz me?" I laugh, and I'm met with the sound of silence. Jerking it from my ear, I look at the caller ID, and it's an unknown number out of the same area code I had in Boston.

"Who is this?" I ask, with a chill running through my bones and the hair standing on the back of my neck.

A deep voice answers, "Wrong number," then hangs up.

All the air is expelled in my lungs in relief. Rolling my shoulders back to alleviate the tension, I focus on my plot, and the words literally fall out. I don't stop until my phone rings again, this time checking the number.

"So you really do know how to call a woman back," I joke.

"I'm on my way to your place."

"Crap! What time is it?" I twist to look at the clock. I've been lost in my story for the past five hours.

"Time for our date."

"I still have to pack a picnic and change clothes."

"Don't worry about food. Mercy jammed leftovers from dinner in a basket for me. I'll see you in ten minutes. Be ready." He disconnects.

I fly through my drawers and can't find anything suitable to wear. "Sage is right. I need a new wardrobe." On to the closet only to come to the same conclusion. "I know," I snap my fingers and run to Sage's bedroom. "She won't mind if I borrow a thing or two."

Choosing a pair of khakis that look like military pants and a black form-fitting long-sleeve T-shirt, I change clothes and then find a pair of black hiking boots. My hair goes in a pony to be tucked through the back of a ball cap. Facing the mirror, I read the print on the hat. *Warning. I have no filter.* It perfectly describes Sage.

I hear Blaise pull up in the driveway in his truck and open the door before he can knock.

His mouth gapes, and his fist is in midair of a knock. "Wow!"

"What?" I scowl, peering down at the clothes I'm wearing.

"How am I supposed to keep my hands to myself with you looking like some badass warrior?"

"Really?" I laugh. "You like this?"

His eyes darken, and he licks his lips with a sexy, smoldering grin. "I do."

Spinning around, I lock the door. "Let's go, cowboy, before we break your new rule," I snort. "Oh, I forgot to grab my gun."

"No need. I have plenty we can work with. It will be good to teach you how to handle a multitude of weapons."

"That strangely scares me and turns me on." I giggle, hopping into his truck.

He climbs inside. "This is going to be way harder than I imagined," he groans.

"Before I forget"—I fasten my seatbelt—"I rented a spot in Katherine's building for Sage's gallery. I want to surprise her when she gets back. Do you think you could lend me a hand and your truck to take some of her canvas photos over and help set up?"

"I'd love to. Just tell me when and where to be."

"Will Sunday work for you?"

"I'll pencil it in my calendar." He smirks. "You're an honest-to-goodness friend. She's going to love it."

"I hope so. She's been weird about it for so long."

"Any idea why?"

"Money, perhaps, or fear of failure. She always wants to be so independent."

"There's nothing wrong with independence."

"Says the man that lives with his family."

"That's strictly out of convenience. Knox is building each of us a place of our own. She got sidetracked having to move from Lola, but she's back on it now."

"Where are you building a house?"

"We all invested in the ranch when we moved from Kentucky. River put in the bulk of the money with the intention of buying us out and giving each of us some acreage."

"Do you plan on opening your own garage one day?"

"No. I love what I do and where I work. I make a decent living and have very few expenses. I'm not the type of man who requires a lot."

"It's great you love your job and life. I can't imagine being anything else other than an author. It's what I was born to do."

"And from what I've read, you're very successful at it."

"You Googled me?" I raise my brows.

"I can't plan on falling in love with a complete stranger." His smile is the broadest I've seen it, melting away any resolve I had about him.

"Love, huh? Do you really think a country boy can mesh with a city girl?" I tease.

"I know nothing about meshing, but I could work the city girl right out of you. Today, you look like a warrior...next, you'll be dressed in plaid."

"Don't count on that." My laughter fills the cab of his Bronco. "Perhaps I'll get you in city boy attire. A nice suit, with skinny-legged pants."

"Not in your wildest dreams. Can you imagine me getting a boner in those polyester pants? I'd be like waving a red flag. At least in jeans, I can hide it."

"You don't do a very good job at that," I mutter from the corner of my mouth.

"How about you remain the city slicker, and I'll stay the Wrangler-wearing cowboy. I think we'll do just fine."

We laugh and banter back and forth until he parks at a small cabin tucked into the side of a mountain.

"I thought we were going to a shooting range?"

"We are. There's one set up behind the hunting cabin."

"Does this belong to you?"

"It came with the ranch. The owner didn't want it, so he threw it in with the deal. Walker and I have been the only ones to use it."

He gets out and grabs a large black bag out of the back seat. "We'll skip the cottage for now and make our way around back before we lose daylight. Plus, we're fighting those gnarly-looking rain clouds. Snag the picnic basket if it's not too heavy."

Hauling the strap of the basket over my shoulder, I follow him to the back of the cottage and set it down on a rugged wooden table that appears to be a permanent part of the outdoor fixtures.

"Sorry. We haven't replaced any of the furniture. We were more focused on setting up the shooting range." He points to targets downrange.

"Don't be sorry. This is awesome. I love the authenticity of it. I bet Sage would love a photo op here."

He digs through the bag and takes out two pistols, a rifle, and a short shotgun. "Have you ever shot anything other than a gun?"

I shake my head.

"Let's see how you do with the pistol first." He hands it to me, and I grip it in both hands.

"I want you to aim at target one, then three."

The first target is a short distance away. The third one sits in a crevice of the stone mountain.

Extending my arms, I hold the gun out.

"Wait," he says and moves in behind me, placing his hands on my forearms. "You need a little give to your elbows. Not loosely, but not so straight either." He positions me like he wants then steps to the side of me.

Squeezing the trigger, I hit the first target.

"Nice," he utters.

Repositioning, I aim at the next target, and it hits the outside area.

"Move a tad to the left," he says, curling his fingers for me to step toward him. "Keep both eyes open and try again."

Doing as he instructs, I nail the target and squeal. "I've never shot that far before."

"You're a quick study. Give it a few more rounds, and we'll move on to the rifle."

With each aim, I get closer and closer until I hit the target directly in the middle.

"I think you're ready." He chuckles. Picking up the rifle he had lying on the table, he walks over to me, showing me how to handle it and the details on each part. Then gives me eye protection and orange-colored foam earplugs. "Do you see the fourth target?" He points up higher into the mountain.

"Yes."

"That's your mark."

"That's pretty far." I peer through the scope.

"Good thing you have a great teacher." He grins and moves behind again.

I don't know if it's the adrenaline flowing through my body or his touch, but his fingertips on my hips send flames of desire between my thighs.

"Keep your stance wide."

I'm keenly aware of his hands moving to my shoulders.

"Stay solid through your middle."

My core is melting with need at the moment. "Okay." My voice sounds raspy even to me.

"You good?" By his tone, I can tell he knows the effect he's having on me.

"Could you maybe not touch me." I laugh, and he smiles.

"I like that I have such a powerful effect on you." He chuckles, releasing me.

"Stance wide, solid core," I repeat, positioning myself. "Keep both eyes open." I squeeze the trigger, and the sound of the bullet leaving the chamber echoes loudly. "Did I hit it?"

"Not even close," he roars. "Try again."

After the fourth time, I barely clip the target when the rain starts falling. We hustle to get the gear, and I grab the basket, jogging to the front of the cabin. He unlocks the door, but we are already drenched. I nearly stumble on the half-rotten porch leading to the warped doorframe.

Shaking the water from my hair and wiping it off of my shoulders, I step inside. It has a wood plank floor with old water spots on it from where the roof has leaked. A rusty kerosene lantern sets by the stone fireplace filled with ash. The only thing new in the place is the gun rack by the door.

"You bring a girl to the nicest places," I snicker. My fingertip comes up black when I run it down a dirty windowsill with flies lying dead in the corner of it. "Are those mouse droppings?" I point.

"More like raccoons."

My head whips around. "Seriously?" My voice has taken flight to a pitch I've never heard, and he chuckles.

"It's mice. I promise." He blatantly crosses his fingers.

"Good thing we are only seeking shelter and not staying the night."

"With the rain letting down, I'm afraid we're not going anywhere." He peeks through an off-white curtain that sends a layer of dust into the air.

"At least tell me where the bathroom is so I can wipe off. You do have towels, right?" I cock a brow.

"I'm afraid it's worse than no towels." He looks totally amused.

"What aren't you telling me?"

"The bathroom is an outhouse on the side of the property."

"You've got to be kidding me."

"Are you bush-trained?"

"I'm...I'm not sure what you're asking me?"

"You could always pee in the bushes if you'd prefer." He's enjoying my torment way too much.

"You do know we hardly have trees in Boston, and I'd get arrested for indecent exposure for peeing on one of them."

"I think you'd prefer it to the outhouse. That's probably where the raccoon is hiding," he teases, I think.

"I'm not liking you very much right about now." I cross my arms and narrow an eye at him.

15

BLAISE

"Damn, you're pretty when you're flustered." My boots thump over the floorboards when I close the gap between us.

The wind blows hard, shaking the old ill-fitted windows, and she jumps. "What's that noise?"

"It's just the storm." I drag her into my arms. "Don't worry, I'll protect you." I chuckle. A draft whistles through the cracks in the walls and down the chimney, and she shivers. I lift her chin with the crook of my finger. "Seriously, we're fine."

"I'm cold, that's all," she tries to hide her fear.

"The last time I came up here, I left some clothes. Why don't you go change, and I'll start us a fire. Then we can dig into the food Mercy packed." I point her in the direction of the room, and she disappears.

Walker and I cut fresh wood on our last visit and stacked it by the fireplace. Brushing out some of the ash, I stack the wood and grab a box of matches off of the mantle, striking it. It lights easily. Taking off my shirt, I lay it in front of the fireplace to dry. When I turn around, Thayer is scowling from the doorway. "You were serious about getting me in plaid."

She's wearing a red and black shirt with a pair of ragged-out overalls that are two sizes too big for her. "Now, that's attractive," I tease.

She moseys across the floor barefooted to the fire. "You did this on purpose, didn't you? And how the heck am I supposed to keep our no-sex deal when you're half naked?"

"At least it's not the lower half, but I could accommodate you if you'd like." I tug at the button on my jeans, but she halts my hand. "I'll deal with you shirtless." She licks her lips, and I want to screw my bad idea.

"What's in the basket? I'm starved. When I get in my writing cave, I forget to eat."

"Fried chicken and biscuits. I threw in a couple bottles of beer to go with it."

"I have to admit, I don't believe I've ever had home-made fried chicken."

I pull out the checkered blanket from the basket and spread it out in front of the fireplace. "You're in for a real treat. Mercy has perfected my grandmother's recipe, and it's the best."

She sits with her legs folded underneath her. "Is your grandmother still alive?"

"No. She died long before we were born, but the way my family always talked about her, I felt like I knew her."

"What are your parents like?"

"Good people. My dad wasn't raised by his father. He and his sister didn't meet the Calhouns until after their mother died. It's a long story that turned out to be one of the best things that ever happened to either one of them. They are all very close-knit. In fact, my mother, Molly, and Aunt Jane, who is Mercy's mom are best friends. My mother was a surrogate for Mercy."

"Wow, that's incredible."

"I've always thought of Mercy more like a sister than a cousin. My sister Eden is two years older than me. Enough about my upbringing. What about you. Do you have any siblings?"

"No. I'm an only child. My mother found out she had breast cancer while she was pregnant with me. She went into remission for several years, but she spent a lot of time fighting it."

"I'm so sorry." I sweep a piece of hair from her face.

"My father, like yours, is a good man. Stern with most people but always very loving and tender with me."

"I'd love to meet the man that's raised such a wonderful woman." Removing the lid from the plastic container, I put the food on the paper plates and uncap the beers. Holding the amber bottle out, I tap it against hers. "Here's to us getting to know one another and me restraining myself from unbuckling your overalls," I add with a smile.

"There is something seriously wrong with you if this outfit turns you on," she hoots.

"It's the woman underneath it that does it for me. You could be wearing a feed sack, and I'd still want to rip it off of you."

She licks her lips and bites off a piece of chicken. "Are you determined you want to maintain this hands-off rule of yours? And, damn, this is good." She smacks her mouth.

"I'm not certain one bit"—I shake my head—"but I am starving." The chicken crunches when I chomp off a piece.

"I'm curious, you being a rancher, I haven't heard you mention having any dogs." She digs into her biscuit with her fingers.

"River has one."

"Do you not like dogs?"

"In my mind, they have an expiration date. I can't handle the thought of losing one, so I chose not to own a dog."

"It's really kind of sad you think in those terms. We're meant to love and lose people, but I'd rather have loved than never have taken a chance."

"Were you in love with Brent?"

"I had feelings for him in the beginning, but I was so young I had no idea what love felt like."

"Do you now?"

"I'm not sure. I tend to doubt my feelings because of him."

"Then you're not so different from me. You protect your heart one way, me another."

"I guess we're perfect for each other." Her eyes twinkle.

I bend and kiss the corners of her mouth. "I'd like to think so. You taste good." I grin.

"This is not a hands-off approach, and with you this close to me, I'm weak. Especially after seeing you manhandle a gun. All that pent-up testosterone is sexy."

"Do you know what I find sexy?" I kiss a trail down her neck.

"Surely not this attire," she snorts, then gasps when my lips find their way inside her plaid top, landing on her collarbone.

"Everything about you," I rasp, not able to control my desire to want her in my bed again, opening her body to mine.

"If you keep this up, I won't be able to stop." Her voice is breathy and full of as much need as I'm feeling.

"I'm a weak, horny man. To hell with my own rule," I hiss. Reaching inside her bra, I cup her breast in the palm of my hand, then suck her nipple into my mouth, teasing it with my tongue into a peak, garnering a loud moan from her lips.

Moving our food to the side with a sweep of my hand, I lay her back and unfasten her overalls as I go and nearly ripping the buttons from the thread, holding them on to open her shirt. When I kiss her neck again, she shivers.

"Are you cold?"

"Quite the opposite," she purrs.

Leaning up, I grasp her overalls at the waist, and she raises her hips. I tug them down her long legs, tossing them to the side, followed by her panties, leaving her bare from the waist down. My lips find the spot between her breasts and move south until I've found the sweet spot between her thighs.

"Blaise," she rasps when I lick her.

With pressure from my thumb on her wet nub, she bucks.

"My cock aches to be inside of you, but I want to draw out every ounce of pleasure I can give you first."

She digs her fingernails into my shoulders and thrusts her hips to my mouth, and moans as I take full advantage of the situation. I lap her up and apply more pressure and feel her body tense as she finds her orgasm. The first of many to follow if I have my way. As soon as her body settles, I go again, bringing on a chain reaction of releases from her.

"Blaise." She says my name as a prayer, thanking me yet wanting so much more.

Climbing her body with kisses until I find her mouth, letting her have a taste of herself, she moans again, wrapping her legs around my hips.

"Take off your jeans," she hisses.

I stand long enough to take them off and then brace my body over hers. "Roll over," I command. "I want to take you from behind." Raising an inch, allowing her to turn.

Spreading her legs with my thighs, my cock fits snuggly in the crack of her ass. I rock my hips back and forth.

"Please, I want you inside," she begs, lifting her ass.

After slipping on a condom, I position my tip at her entrance and slowly...inch by inch...dip inside her until I'm fully seated, and she clamps down around me. I hold my breath, riding out her orgasm, trying like hell not to blow it. A fine sheen of sweat covers her body, and she shivers again when I kiss my way up her spine to the crook of her neck, snaking my hands to her breast.

"You feel amazing," I say, tenderly firmly planted against her skin. Then in one move, I bolt back to my knees, taking her with me. We are both on our knees, and I pull her into my lap and bury myself yet deeper. Her head falls back, and her hair trails down my chest.

"You're so deep," she moans.

"Am I hurting you?"

"Only in a good way." She twists her neck to find my lips and wraps her hand around the back of my neck.

"I'm going to move, and when I do, it's going to be rough. Are you okay with that?"

"More than okay," she pants.

I take her hands and plant them on the floor in front of her, then grip her hips, wanting to sheath her in one ruthless thrust, yet at the same time wanting to drag out slow gasps of pleasure from her. She feels amazing, like I was made to fit perfectly with her warmth snuggly around me, not wanting to be anywhere else but with her. My brain says go slow, but the aching in my dick wins out, and I repeatedly move in and out of her. I snake my hand underneath her, touching her folds, then I drive inside her over and over until she screams my name.

"Blaise!"

A need to claim her fills me, and I root deeper than I've ever been. She, along with every muscle in her body, screams with satisfaction without her knowing her acceptance of relenting to me makes her mine. The squeezing of my chest with the thought never happens. She tightens around my cock, and I release deep inside her.

We go to the floor when I reluctantly pull out of her, and she rolls to face me. "Are you alright?" Her hand cups my face.

"I'm good. Did I hurt you?"

"Not at all. I meant emotionally are you okay?" She blinks a few times.

"All I could think about was how much I wanted you, and I don't believe that feeling is going to change." I swallow my admission hard. "You're mine, and I don't ever want to share you or be with another woman."

"I don't know whether I broke you or fixed you," she says softly.

"I know one part of my body you broke," I jest and rock my already hardening again cock to her belly.

"It doesn't appear to be too broken." She giggles.

"You've tamed my heart."

"As long as I didn't subdue the wild side of you that makes you...you." She splays her hand over my chest. "You're sweet, funny, and have a spark for life, whether you realize it or not, hidden by the darkness inside of you. I want to keep you wild and make that darkness disappear as long as you're only wild for me," she adds.

I press my forehead to hers but keep my gaze connected to hers. "Right now, in this moment, it's the only thing I want. I can't promise old ghosts won't rear their ugly heads on occasion, but I can assure you, I won't be in anyone else's arms but yours. You've single-handedly spun my world off of its axis."

She pushes me onto my back and straddles me. "Now that we've settled that, I want my turn." She strokes the length of my shaft.

"Can you do that thing you described in your book I'm reading? The one in chapter seventeen." I grin.

She smiles right before she leans down, pressing a kiss to the tip of my cock. "I most certainly can."

16

THAYER

"Damn, girl. I don't think I've ever seen you smile so much." Sage's body is angled toward me and pointing in my direction from the driver's side of my car.

"I'm honestly happy. Thank you for convincing me to move halfway across the world."

"Ah, Blaise put that look of happiness on your face. I bet that cowboy gave you the best sex of your life."

"Sage!" I howl.

"Don't act all innocent with me. I've read your books," she snorts.

"He's so much more than I thought the first time I laid eyes on him. I really like him."

"I'm excited for you. Where are we going, by the way?" She scowls when we pass the road to our house.

"I have a surprise for you, something that Blaise has been helping me with."

She claps her hands. "You've found me a hot cowboy."

"I wouldn't dare. You'd eat him alive." I laugh. Turning onto Main Street, I park outside the building.

"Isn't this Katherine's place?"

I grin but don't respond as I get out of the car. Katherine is tucked into the crook of Walker's arm at the entrance, holding out a key. "I believe you're going to need this," she says.

"I don't understand." Sage frowns.

Walker opens the door, and I place my hands on her shoulders, moving her inside and directing her to her new gallery.

Her eyes grow wide. "What is this?"

"You've done so much for me, I wanted to do something special for you."

She walks slowly inside, touching every photo. "This is my gallery?"

"Yes. No more excuses."

"But I can't afford this."

"Your rent has been paid for one year. All you have to do is keep taking amazing photos," Katherine says and holds a print from her wedding. Sage had sent her a link to the photos before she left town. "This black-and-white print is my favorite."

She's holding a candid picture Sage snapped when Walker was gazing into her eyes on the dance floor. Pure love and affection danced in his eyes, and I recall when she shared it, telling me she'd never been so completely jealous that a woman could be so loved in a single look.

"I can't believe you did this for me." Her eyes well up with tears.

"You like it?"

"Yes, of course." She hugs me.

"Good. Because I thought several times you might be upset that I did all of this without your consent."

"It's the push I needed. We're going to have to have an official art gallery opening," she squeals. "This is absolutely amazing. Better than I ever imagined it would be."

"Blaise was a big help in setting things up."

"Where is your hunka hunka burning love?"

I roar in laughter. "He wanted to be here, but he had to help drive the cattle today."

"Thank you so much for all of this." She waves her hand around. "I love the floating wall. It gives me room to display more prints."

"We'll bring a case of champagne for opening night," Walker states. "This town is going to love your work."

"I have one more surprise for you," I say, taking her hand. I lead her to the back of the gallery and open a door. "Blaise had a great idea."

She flips on the light. "A dark room." She clutches her chest, and the tears that were threatening to be released fall. "I don't have to develop pictures out of a closet in our house anymore."

"You've worked hard and deserve it."

"This is too much." She crushes me in her arms. "I'll have to give that cowboy of yours a big smooch."

"As long as it's on the cheek. I'm a jealous woman," I snort.

"I truly can't thank you enough. Left up to me, I'd be working out of my house forever and never sharing my prints with the world other than online."

"You're going to be such a success, my friend. I love you."

"I love you too."

Walker's phone pings, and he looks at it. "Excuse me, I have to take this." He steps away, leaving Katherine's side for the first time.

"So, how was the honeymoon?" I ask.

"I never wanted it to end," she beams.

"I bet your son missed you."

"Knox and Greer kept him so busy I don't think he gave us a second thought."

"I've gotten to know them a little bit, and they are a great family."

"The best," she chimes. "One big protective, ornery, loving bunch."

My heart warms thinking about the past several days in Blaise's arms, making love in the middle of the night and waking up for more of the same. He's never made me feel like he wants to bolt, and he makes sure I know it. The one morning he had to leave before dawn, he wrote a note on my mirror with my pink lipstick telling me he wasn't going to break my heart because I had stolen his and it was off the market. The message is still there, reminding me. He's something I never knew I wanted or needed, and he's tilted my world as much as I have his.

Walker comes back in and whispers something in Katherine's ear, and she gasps.

"Is everything alright?" Sage asks.

"We have to go to the hospital. Mercy took a fall."

"Is she the one that's pregnant?" Sage scowls.

"Yeah, she's six months along, and I guess it was a pretty hard spill. She lost consciousness."

"Go." She shoos them away.

"Do you mind if I tag along?" I ask Walker.

"I'm sure Blaise would like you to be there." He sweetly lays his hand on my shoulder. "I know he comes across as someone that's tough, but he's always had a soft spot for Mercy."

"He told me he thinks of her as a sister and why."

Walker grins. "He did, did he?"

"Yes," I respond slowly.

"Blaise must really like you. He doesn't give much about himself." He walks between his wife and me, ushering us out of the building.

I get in my car and follow them to the hospital. As soon as Blaise lays eyes on me, he rushes over, wrapping his arms around me. He smells like dust and dirt and has a smudge on his chin.

"What happened?" I draw back, looking him in the eye.

"From what Greer said, she was at the top of the stairs and complained of feeling light-headed. Greer tried to get her to sit, but she insisted it would pass, and she lost her footing and fell down the stairs. Greer said it took a good five minutes to arouse her, and she was confused.

"She called Atley, and she sent an ambulance. I heard it hauling ass down toward the main house, and I rode like hell off of the mountain to see what happened. I was bringing up the tail end of the herd and didn't even tell them I was leaving. I radioed Hardin as soon as I saw Mercy. He's in there with her now."

"Are the others still out on the cattle drive?" Walker braces his shoulders.

"Yeah, they couldn't just leave them. They'll be here as soon as they can."

"There isn't anything I can do for her here. I'm going to go see if I can lend them a hand. You stay here," he tells Katherine.

"I should go with you," Blaise chokes out.

"It's more important for you to be here. We'll handle the cattle."

Blaise presses his lips together and nods. "Alright. I'll call you as soon as we hear anything about her condition."

Walker kisses his wife and marches out of the waiting room.

"How about I go get everyone some coffee?" I offer.

Knox is pacing with Greer, who I hear blaming herself for not insisting on stopping Mercy.

"Just stay right here with me," Blaise tucks me under his chin. "Mercy and Hardin had a hard time conceiving. If she loses this baby..." His pain lodges in his throat.

"Don't think like that. Babies have lots of cushion and are tougher than we think."

"She'd never be the same, and I don't want that kind of pain for her or Hardin to endure."

"Don't go there." I take his face in my hands. "Do you hear me?"

He licks a tear from his lips.

Both our heads turn when Atley strolls into the waiting room. "Mercy is pretty battered, but the baby seems to be okay. We're going to do a few more tests and keep her for a couple of days to make sure things don't change. My advice will be bed rest for several weeks."

"So the baby is out of danger?" Blaise asks.

"At the moment, yes, but sometimes injuries don't show up right away, and how Mercy's body is going to react, we don't know. I'm thankful her water didn't break, but she could still go into premature labor, and it's way too early for the baby to come into this world. But I promise she and her baby will get the best care, and I'm going to do everything I can to make sure the baby stays where he belongs."

"He?" Knox states.

"I probably shouldn't have let that slip." She cringes.

"Mercy is having a son," Blaise repeats. "When can we see her?"

"Hardin is at her side, but I'm sure he wouldn't mind if one of you peeked in on her."

Without questioning, Knox and Greer seem to know Blaise needs to be the one. "You go," Greer says. "And you tell her when she's better, I'm going to kick her ass," she sniffs.

"I think you'll have to stand in line behind Hardin." He half laughs.

"Thanks for staying, but as soon as I'm done here, I'm going back to the ranch. I'll call you later."

"Are you sure you're okay?" I whisk a piece of hair from his forehead. I can't help but have a twinge of fear with the lost look in his eyes.

He never answers. "I'll call you later," he repeats, then stomps through the door, following Atley.

"You're good for him," Knox says, coming close to me. "I've never seen him smile so much."

"He's had the same effect on me."

"I don't think you understand how special you are. We all assumed he was a lost cause when it came to his heart, but you've woken a beast in him that's glorious to see."

"I just hope he can rein in the sadness buried in his eyes."

"The one thing I've learned about Blaise is that he's very good at hiding his pain. The fact that you see it reassures me of how he feels about you and you him. I heard this quote once, 'only those that care about you can hear you when you're quiet.' That's how I know you truly love him, whether either one of you are ready to admit it or not."

She hugs me and walks back over to Greer, and her comment plays in my mind as I walk back to my car. I think I fell in love with him the moment I laid eyes on him. I only hope he doesn't break me.

I drive to the gallery to find Sage, but as I'm getting out, my phone rings, snatching it to my ear. "Is she alright?"

"I don't know who she is," a deep voice responds.

"Who is this?" I look at the number on my phone, and it's the same one that came in as a wrong number several days ago.

"The man you can't get away from so easily."

Every fiber of my being stands tall, and I shake uncontrollably, hanging up. "Why can't you just leave me alone!" I scream. My head spins as I walk into the gallery and press my fingertips to my temples.

"What's wrong?" Sage asks, rushing over to me.

I don't want to ruin this day for her, and she'll go ballistic. "Nothing more than being concerned about Mercy." I straighten my shoulders and suck in my fear.

"Did she lose the baby?"

"No, but they are admitting her to make sure she doesn't."

"Sounds like a good plan."

"Yes, she's in good hands. Now, what can I do to help you?"

"You've done enough already," she snorts. "I can't thank you enough."

"When do you want to do an official opening?"

"I'll do a soft opening in a couple of weeks, but I want to do a larger one in a few months when I get everything set up perfectly. We could include a book signing for you. The people in this town need to know your name."

That's the last thing I want right now, to advertise my whereabouts. "No, I want this to be one hundred percent about you. I don't need the exposure."

"Are you worried he might find you?"

He already has. "I'd rather just keep a low profile."

"Understandable." That seems to appease her. "I want to take you out to lunch to celebrate."

"I'm all in for a round of margaritas." We lock arms and barrel down the sidewalk to the brewery.

17

BLAISE

"You scared the hell out of all of us," I mutter, kissing Mercy's forehead.

"She won't be doing that anymore. I'm putting her on lockdown until the baby is born." Hardin's tone sparks with rigidness.

"I have to admit, I was pretty frightened." She rubs her baby bump. "I should have used the good sense God gave me and just sat down."

"Yes, you should have." Hardin glares at her with his arms crossed over his chest.

She reaches out and lays her hand on his forearm, and his eyes soften. "I'm sorry, and I'll be more careful," she sniffs.

"I'm going to give the two of you a few minutes alone and go find Atley." He leans down, placing a gentle kiss to her lips. "I love you and our son," he states, then hustles out the door.

"Atley let it slip that you're having a boy," I say, sitting on the edge of her bed.

"We're going to name him after my father."

"Uncle Ethan will love it. Does he know you took a spill?"

"Hardin spoke with him, and then I got a video lecture from him, and I had to talk him down so he didn't hop on the next plane headed here."

"Knowing him and Aunt Jane, they ignored your plea." I chuckle.

"You're probably right." She rests her head back on the pillow. "I just don't want them fussing over me."

"It's what parents do, and I'm sure one day you'll do the same thing for your son."

"How are you?" she asks, rubbing the scowl on my brow with her thumb.

"I'm alright, but you had me worried. The thought of losing you is unbearable."

"Hey," she says tenderly, "you're not going to lose me. Don't go getting that notion stuck in that thick head of yours."

"I'll try not to." A smile quirks on my lips.

"Thayer looks good on you. I'm happy you found her."

"Me too..." I stand and walk to the foot of her bed.

"Don't do it!" She points. "This was my accident. Don't apply it to Thayer. Nothing is going to happen to her."

I turn my gaze away from her, scratching the side of my head. "I want to believe that so badly because I'm crazy in love with her."

"Have you told her yet?"

"No."

"You should."

Bracing my hands on the footboard, I exhale. "If I speak the words, it will end."

"Why do you think that?" She sits tall and scowls.

"Because the day I spoke those words to Rachel, she hung herself."

"Thayer is not Rachel. She's a successful woman that has her act together. Rachel was a young, tormented girl who knew no other way out."

"How do I know Thayer isn't the same way? Rachel hid it well."

"Oh, sweetie," she says, patting the bed. "Come back here and sit." When I do, she continues. "I bet if you take a hard look back at the situation, there were signs, and you have to quit comparing the two. I'm sure your therapist has gone over this with you."

"She has, but I still feel the weight of the guilt of it all."

"That guilt that you've tucked away is what's holding you back. Rachel's choice took so much away from you, and you have to find a way to not blame yourself. When that happens, you'll be set free. In the meantime, don't throw your relationship away with Thayer because you're scared to love someone."

"I came here to lecture you, and you're the one giving me advice," I scoff.

"Believe me, my lecture from my normally very sweet husband was harsh."

"I don't blame him one bit."

Neither one of us hears Hardin enter the room. "I wasn't angry. Terrified of losing you and our baby, but not angry."

I stand, and Mercy holds out her hand. "I know."

"I'm going to get out of here and let you rest and get back to the cattle."

"Thanks, man," Hardin says. "I'm sure they could use your help."

"You have your hands full with this one." I laugh, clapping him on the shoulder.

"You remember what I said," Mercy hollers as I walk into the hallway.

"I will. And you listen to whatever Atley tells you to do," I respond.

"Don't worry, she will," Hardin states.

* * *

Driving the herd kept my brain preoccupied because I was feeling like a part of me died inside today with the thought of losing Mercy. I've shaken the idea off a million times and let my fear roll down in the bottom of the shower along with the dirt and grim on my skin.

I make it to Thayer's just as she is climbing into bed. "You okay," she asks, letting me in the door.

"Yeah. Do you mind if I hold you?"

She tucks her hands around my waist and tilts her chin toward mine. "I never mind being held by you."

Placing my hand on the small of her back with a need to touch her, we walk to her bedroom, and I strip out of my clothes down to my boxers. She climbs underneath the covers, and I get in next to her with my chest to her back and hold her tight.

"Do you want to talk?" she asks, barely above a whisper.

"No. I have what I want in my arms." I kiss her shoulder. "Get some rest."

It isn't long before she dozes off. I lie for hours, drifting in and out of sleep with no desire to release her from my arms, instead holding her as close to me as I possibly can. "I want no distance between us," I speak quietly in her ear. "I love you." My heart races with an unfounded fear of losing her. My lips find the soft skin of her neck, and I breathe in her scent. She's the most intoxicating thing in the world to me. Her velvety skin feels so smooth against my lips. My fingers itch, hungering to roam over her body, but I stifle them, not wanting to wake her. She's given herself freely to a man who doesn't deserve her trust, and my cock aches, yearning to sheath myself in her tight body. I've never felt desire so badly, feeling like I'll never have enough of her, but live in fear of losing her. She's gutted me with a thirst to love and protect her, even from myself and my mixed-up emotions. There's not an ounce of me that wants to resist her, unlike any other woman I've ever been with.

She moves, and I and my cock remain stock-still. Rolling in my arms, she's still asleep, burying her nose against my neck. I tuck a strand of hair behind her ear, and she says my name.

"Blaise." Her eyes remain closed, and I hold her until my lids follow suit. When I open them again, she's staring at me with an adorable grin.

"Good morning," she rasps.

I blink a few times. "Morning. What time is it?"

"Seven."

"Damn. I gotta go." I throw back the sheet.

"I was hoping I could help you take care of that tenting in your boxers." She licks her lips.

"As much as I'd love to say yes, I'm expecting a crucial part for a piece of equipment that I have to get running this morning."

"I had a dream last night that you told me you loved me." She grabs my hand.

It wasn't a dream, but if I admit it out loud... "Sounds like the perfect dream," I say, leaning in for a kiss. "I'll call you later."

She exhales. "If it were true, I wouldn't mind it."

"Can we talk about this later? I've really got to go."

"I'm going to hold you to it," she hollers as I head out the door.

Instead of driving to the ranch, I swerve into the parking lot of my therapist's office when I see her car parked out front. Her door is cracked open, so I let myself inside.

"You're getting an early start this morning." She jumps when she hears my voice.

"You startled me." She clasps her chest.

"I'm sorry," I mutter, running my hand through my bedhead. "I saw your car out front, and I was hoping you'd have a minute."

"If you're standing in front of me this early in the morning, I can only assume you really need to talk." She waves toward the chair.

"Something happened yesterday that has me retreating into my darkness, and I can't seem to shake it."

"Tell me." She takes her usual seat.

"My cousin Mercy fell down the stairs, and she's six months pregnant."

"Did she lose the baby?"

"No. She was lucky. She's a little beat up, but the baby seems to be fine."

"That's good news, so why are you struggling?"

"Because she could have died."

"But she didn't, and you and I both could die walking across the street."

"Yes, but..."

"Are you taking your medication?"

"I may have forgotten a few doses." I shrug.

"It will keep you on an even keel and help you deal with your irrational fear of someone dying."

"Yeah, but it makes me feel like a zombie."

"That's a common complaint. I could try you on a different medication, but unfortunately the side effects are the same."

I stand. "You're right. It's irrational."

"You saying it doesn't make your feelings go away. Focus on being grateful that everything turned out okay. How are things going with Thayer?"

I return to my seat. "So well it's scary."

"Embrace how you're feeling, don't run from it."

"I told her I loved her when I thought she was sleeping."

"That's a huge breakthrough for you, but try saying it when she's awake." She laughs.

"When she woke this morning, she said she had a dream that I told her that I loved her, so she heard me."

"How did you respond?"

"I tucked my tail and left and showed up on your doorstep." I chuckle.

"Tell her," she urges. "You can do this, and I promise you'll start to let go of the past, which is long overdue."

"I will. Tonight." I slap my knee and get to my feet.

"Call me if you need me to talk you through it."

"Thanks. I'll keep you on speed dial." I smile.

"Good luck, Blaise. I mean it. I have a feeling you won't need me much longer, which relates to me doing a good job with you."

"You've been a very patient woman," I quip and close the door behind me.

The delivery truck is already at the garage when I arrive, and Hardin is signing for the part.

"Sorry I'm late." I take the box from him. "How are Mercy and the baby?"

"I spoke with Atley first thing this morning, and both mom and baby are doing well. Mercy talked her into letting her come home, but only if she agrees to bed rest until further advised. We're going to stay in her old bedroom so she can have plenty of help while I'm working. Norah says she's not letting her out of her sight."

"I pity Norah's job. Mercy is a handful."

"She only has to keep her settled until tomorrow when her parents arrive."

"I knew Aunt Jane and Uncle Ethan would head out to Montana. Her father is about the only person I know she'll listen to other than you."

"She ain't even good at that," he howls.

"Mercy loves you, even if she is hardheaded."

"I know she does. I'm not the easiest person to deal with either. I'd say we're perfect for one another."

"I couldn't agree more. You're lucky to have each other."

"Mercy told me about Thayer. Sounds like things are coming up roses for the two of you."

"I sure hope so."

"Hope isn't a strategy, man. If you love her, forget about all the other crap and make it happen."

"You sound like my therapist."

"I'll send you my bill." He laughs. "I have to check on the men before I go pick up my wife and bring her home. I'll see you later."

"Tell her I'll talk to her this afternoon."

"Will do."

18

THAYER

"I'm sorry. I'm not available for book signings anytime soon," I tell my publisher, who isn't too happy about it. "I'm keeping a low profile these days. You're aware of my situation, so please try to understand. I don't need to announce my whereabouts in public." She doesn't need to know he's already contacted me, but there is one person I need to speak with, and I'm parked outside of his office building.

Hanging up, I get out and take the sidewalk to the entryway of the sheriff's department. I'm greeted by a woman at the front desk. "May I help you?" she asks, peering over the rim of her glasses.

"I'd like to speak to Sheriff Calhoun if that's possible."

"Do you have an appointment with him?"

"No...I..."

"Thayer," Chase says my name from his office doorway, waving me inside. "It's alright. I'll see her," he tells the lady.

"Thank you." I amble to his office, and he greets me with a handshake.

"What can I do for you?"

"Can I shut the door," I ask, pointing at it.

"By all means." He sits behind his desk. "Blaise advised me on your stalker. I can only assume if you're in my office, he contacted you in some fashion."

"He did, but I don't want Blaise to know Brent contacted me."

"Why not?" He rests back in his seat and folds his hands in his lap.

"I don't want him to worry about me. He's got enough on his plate already." I sit.

"Blaise would want to know, and he'll be angry if you don't share it with him."

"Yes, but I'm asking you to keep this between the two of us for now."

"As long as I feel like I can protect you. How did he contact you?"

"He called my phone." I hand it to him. "It's a Boston number. The first time he called, he claimed it was a wrong number."

"So he's called you more than once?"

"Twice. The second time he said he was the man I couldn't get away from so easily."

"Have you seen him?"

"No. I don't think he knows where I am yet, but it's only a matter of time."

He presses a button on his phone and asks someone to come into his office. "I'm going to see what our guy can do with this number." When his man comes into the office, he gives him my phone, telling him what he needs and to return it once he's downloaded the information.

"I'll make some calls to see who I can speak with in Boston. Unfortunately, until he shows his face in Montana, there isn't much I can do, and even then, unless he trespasses on your property, my hands will be tied. Do you have a security system in your home?"

"I don't."

"It's something you might want to seriously consider. I can recommend a company for you, but if you'd tell Blaise, he'd have it installed by the end of the day."

"I'm sure I'm overreacting." I stand. "Just because he called me doesn't mean he knows where I live, and I highly doubt he'd come all this way."

"You're a public figure. It wouldn't be too difficult to track you down. And I read the report on Brent. He's a sick bastard, and you can't dismiss him because of the distance. Men like him won't stop until they have what they want, and sadly that person is you."

"I took precautions when I moved here. There is nothing with my physical address on it."

"Doesn't mean he can't figure out what town you're in. Did you change your phone number after the ordeal?"

"Yes."

"And yet, he's called you." His chair creaks when he lays his arms on his desk. "If he can get your private phone number, he'll find you. I'm not trying to frighten you, but I've had experience with his type." He opens his desk drawer and hands me a business card. "Call this security team."

"If I do, Blaise will know something happened."

"Better he know than find your dead body."

"That would crush him." I bite my bottom lip.

"It would do more than that. It would end him, and I'll do everything in my power to not let that happen, including letting him in on our conversation. The one thing you have to know about the Calhouns is that we're very loyal to one another. We'd die to save each other, and that includes you because you hold Blaise's heart in the palm of your hand. That makes you one of us by default."

Chase is calm but resolute, yet has a softness in the corners of his eyes. He's fierce, but I can tell he's a very loving man. "I'll tell Blaise."

He stands, walking me to the desk of the man that has my phone. "Do you have what you need?"

The guy nods, handing the cell phone to me.

"I'll let you know what we find out. In the meantime, keep your eyes peeled for anything suspicious, and call me immediately with any updates. Day or night, it doesn't matter." He rests his hand gently on my shoulder.

"Thank you."

He follows me to the double glass doors and holds one open for me. "I mean it. Don't hesitate to call me." Sincerity is laced in his tone and the creases of his eyes.

Climbing behind the wheel of my car, I drive home and bury myself in work, losing all track of time. I nearly fall over in my chair when there's a knock at the door. Peeking through the blinds, I see Blaise.

"Are you going to let me in?" he asks.

Twisting the deadbolt, I ease the door open, and he steps inside, taking off his Stetson. "Hey." He smiles sweetly, and then his brows dip together. "What's wrong?"

"Nothing. I was lost in writing and didn't hear you drive up, that's all." I'm not ready to tell him just yet.

"Have you eaten anything today?"

"Um...I...no."

"I'm starved. We can either go out, or I can order us a pizza."

"Pizza sounds delicious." I close the door, and he tugs the phone from his back pocket and calls the local pizza house.

"Did you get the parts you needed?" I ask, sitting on the couch.

"Yep. I had it up and running before noon." He joins me and angles his frame toward me. "I have something I need to say." His cheek draws between his teeth.

"What is it? You're worrying me."

"Your dream wasn't a dream."

I beam. "You mean the one where you told me you loved me?"

"That would be the one." His lips press together.

My gaze stays on him. "You're afraid to say those words, aren't you?" I run my hands through the side of his hair.

He shakes his head.

"It's alright. As long as you show me, I don't need to hear the words." I meet my lips with his for a gentle kiss.

He places his hands on my shoulders and holds me at arm's length, staring me in the eyes. "I'm not going to let fear win out and risk losing you. "I love you, Thayer Hawkins. We haven't known each other very long, but there is no doubt in my mind how I feel about you. Since the day you stepped into my life, I've known it even when I tried to deny it. There's a force between us that I don't claim to understand, but it's undeniably present, and I want to give into it completely."

"Wow. For a man that's afraid to share his feelings, I'd say you did a damn good job of it." My eyes fill with tears. "I love you, too, and I feel the same way. I wasn't looking for you, but I'm glad we found each other." Our lips clash in a passionate kiss, and his love for me is evident in the way he swipes his tongue, tasting me.

He stands and lifts me in his arms, carrying me to my bedroom. Placing me on my feet, I weave my hands underneath his shirt to feel his skin. He lifts his arms in the air, and I slip his shirt off, and he grins for a split second until he sees the business card on the corner of my desk. He reaches over, picking it up.

"Chase hands these cards out," he grits out.

"Don't be angry." I take a step back.

"What aren't you telling me? And why the hell didn't you come to me first?" His voice grows stern.

"Brent called my cell phone, and I thought Chase might be able to put a stop to it."

"I'll fucking kill him if he comes near you!" His face reddens.

"I knew this is how you'd react, and I didn't want to tell you until it was necessary."

"I'd call this necessary." He aims a single finger at the floor. "Pack your bags. You're moving to the ranch where I know you'll be safe."

"I'm not doing any such thing. I'm not living my life in fear of him again. Chase is on it, and I'll call to have security set up here."

He dials the number on the card. "Hey, Tim, this is Blaise Calhoun. I need a favor. I'm going to text you an address that needs to have a monitored security system installed ASAP. I'll pay double to have it up and running tomorrow."

"Blaise." I touch his arm, and he raises his hand to hush me.

"That's perfect. Thank you. I'll see you tomorrow," he says, hanging up.

"You didn't have to do that."

He exhales and places his hands on my hips. "Part of loving someone is making sure they're safe."

I kiss his cheek, resolved to accept what he needs to give me. "Thank you. I feel safer already just by being in your arms."

"I couldn't bear it if something happened to you." He trails his lips over my collarbone.

"Something is happening to me right now, and you're the cause of it." My skin heats up under his touch.

His tongue darts out and licks my lips before seizing my bottom lip between his teeth gently, stirring his cock between us. "I need to be inside of you so damn badly it hurts."

"And that's where I want you to be." I hurry out of my clothes along with him and lay back on the bed, spreading my legs for him.

His fingers feather my folds. "You're so wet," he hisses, and his eyes hood with darkness.

A wild fever of desire ripples through my veins, looking at his body. It's perfection, and his saluting cock is beautiful. I have a deep ache that only he can satisfy. He inserts an erotic exploring finger, and I tighten around it, drawing in its pleasure far surpassing a simple want for him. "I need you." I can't keep the words from exploding from my mouth.

He rips open a foil packet and rolls the condom down his length as my mouth waters. His fingers dig into my thighs, dragging my ass to the edge of the bed, and I dang near come with the look he's giving me. Teasing me again with his skilled fingers before he thrusts deep inside me.

"Never say I don't meet your needs," he rasps.

I squirm, eager for him to move faster, but he takes his time, drawing out every ounce of desire for him. Arching impatiently, I hook my heels around his muscular ass, needing more penetration.

His piercing gaze trespasses on pure lust. His movements are deliberate and achingly slow. "I want to feel you."

"Take off the condom," I insist. "I'm on the pill."

He stills. "Are you sure?"

I raise one brow and nod. "I don't want anything between us."

Easing out, he tosses the condom on the floor, then he notches the tip of his cock at my entrance, toying with me, and a loud whimper escapes from my lips. "Please," I beg, feeling completely at his mercy. He unravels me when I feel him skin on skin, deep inside me. He briefly closes his eyes like he's reining in his control.

"You feel so tight," he utters and swallows hard.

The love I'm feeling for him in this moment makes it hard to breathe. When he opens his eyes, he fills me over and over again, my body stretching to accommodate him. His cock hits that sweet spot, and I fist the sheets in my hands, hanging on for dear life. With every thrust, he manages it over and over again until I'm spiraling out of control, satisfying the delicious ache I have for him and him alone. Every stroke has my orgasm looming. I cry out when I spasm around him, caging his hips tightly with my thighs. His chest muscles ripple, propelling an unyielding rhythm as he powers deep inside of me. Another climax courses through me so strongly that I lose my voice.

He curses as his jaw clenches, and he thrusts deeper yet one more time before his cock throbs his release. He collapses to his arms braced over me, staring me in the eyes as waves of aftershocks tremble between us.

I capture his mouth with mine and thread my

fingers through his damp hair. "That was intoxicating."

A smile slowly covers his face. "Nothing like it, and if
you give me a minute or two, we can do it again."

19

BLAISE

"I've never felt so fully loved." She toys with the fine hairs on my chest. "Don't think I don't appreciate how monumental it was for you to tell me those three sweet, glorious words." Her smile reaches from ear to ear.

I roll, turning her to her back. "I meant it. I love you."

"I think you proved it repeatedly," she purrs, running her ankle down the back of my thigh.

"You are beautiful," my teeth lightly graze the flesh of her neck. "You own me. Every...single...inch...of... me." I nip her between my words.

"I'm yours." She has a lusty rasp to her voice, and I like the way I affect her. She digs her fingernails into my back.

"If I don't stop, I'll never get anything done," I hiss, and in one move, I'm on my feet.

"I can't believe you're leaving me." She pouts.

"I've been in your bed for hours, and the security team is due here any minute, so unless you'd like them to find you naked and me buried deep between your legs, I suggest you get that sexy ass of yours out of bed."

"If I must," she says dramatically with the back of her hand pressed to her forehead, and I laugh. She tosses back the sheets. "Do you really think I have a sexy ass?"

"Have you seen it?" I snort.

She peers over her shoulder ."It looks like a typical ass to me."

"Nothing about you even comes close to average." I swat her in the behind with my shirt before I pull it over my head.

"You're the one with a killer body." She sweeps her hand on my chest between me and my shirt, halting me from tucking it in. I drop my lips to hers with every intent of peeling off the jeans I just tugged on. A knock at the door stops me.

"Damn it," I mutter against her lips. "Get dressed."

I hustle out of the room and run into Sage in the hallway. "Who would be here this early?" She yawns.

"It's a security alarm team I hired to get this place secure."

"Did something happen?" Her eyes widen.

"You'll have to ask your roomie." I open the door and shake hands, and step outside to assess the needs of the property.

He makes some suggestions which I'm all for, and then we enter the house to find Sage pacing the floor and Thayer pouring a cup of coffee. "You should have told me the minute he called you," Sage is giving her what for.

"I didn't want to alarm anyone until I knew for sure it was him, and then I went to the sheriff's office."

"You failed to come to me," I scold her, and Sage points between us.

"What he said," she adds.

"Clearly, that's all been rectified, or there wouldn't be a security system being installed." She waves her hand around. "I don't know which one of you is more protective."

Sage and I say "Me" at the same time.

"I'm not going to be a prisoner in my home by either one of you," she snarls and slams her bedroom door.

"I think she's pissed." Sage scrunches her nose.

"I don't give a shit if she's angry. Her safety is all I care about." I focus on the plans he has of the house, and we lay out where cameras need to be installed and a silent alarm.

"I'll go to the warehouse and bring back everything I need. It will be installed by the end of the day," he says, and I let him out. I hightail it to Thayer's room, where I find her in the shower.

"May I join you?" I ask her through the steamed door.

She slides it open, facing me. "I meant what I said. I was held prisoner in my own home because of him, terrified to go anywhere." She's scowling, and by her tone, I know she means business.

I untuck my T-shirt.

"Stop," she says.

"Is that what you really want?" I lift a brow.

She licks her lips. "Maybe."

I grin and yank off my shirt and kick out of my boots.

"I want to shower alone." She slides the door shut.

"I could wash the parts you can't reach."

"I'm more than capable of washing myself." I see her lower her hand between her legs, and my dick hardens.

I suck in a sharp breath. "Wouldn't you rather it be me driving into you?" Unbuttoning my jeans, I let them fall to the floor along with my boxers. "I'll give you whatever you want."

The door inches open. Her gaze trails down my body, and she licks her lips.

"Bloody hell. Are you going to let me in there with you or not?" I squeeze my eyes closed.

"Stop talking," she moans.

Opening my eyes, I see her crooking her finger for me to step inside. "Come here, and none of this sweet stuff."

My brow flares upward. "Is that your ladylike way of asking me to fuck you?"

"Yes, Blaise! Yes!" A jagged breath leaves her.

"Far be it for me not to give the woman I love what she wants." I step inside and close the door.

* * *

"Are you supposed to be out of bed?" I catch Mercy walking around in her bedroom.

"Don't tell Hardin." She rushes back to bed. "Or Norah. I think she's worse than he is."

"River should be back with your parents from the airport any minute."

"It will be so good to have them here, but I wish it was under different circumstances. I hate when they fuss over me."

"Just let them. Soon you'll have this baby and your time will be consumed. Take the R and R."

"Speaking of breaks, you've been MIA a lot lately at night."

"I've been filling my time in a good way." I grin.

"I'm so freaking happy for you."

"I never thought I'd love someone like I do Thayer. No other woman exists for me."

"It's a great feeling when you find your soul mate, isn't it."

"Indeed it is, and I fell for her so quickly. Now, I can't imagine a world without her in it."

"That's how I feel about Hardin."

"That man deserves a gold star for putting up with you," I scoff, and she punches me in the arm. "The same could be said for Thayer."

The sound of footsteps barreling up the stairs has me facing the door.

"There she is," her mother squeals, running to her side for a hug. Uncle Ethan moves in behind her, and then I take a step back when I see my father's face.

"What the heck?" I walk over and hug him.

"Uncle Noah. I didn't know you were coming with my parents," Mercy says between hugs.

"I wanted to see what my son has been up to. You're looking good," he says, bracing his hands on my shoulders.

"It's so nice to see you. Did Mom come with you?"

"No. She wanted to, but she's been fighting a cold and didn't want to risk getting Mercy sick."

"How long are you in town for?"

"Are you trying to get rid of me already?"

"No. Not at all. I have someone I'd like you to meet."

"Someone as in a woman?" He raises both of his brows.

"Yes," I say.

"You're going to love her," Mercy adds.

"She must be special if you're wanting to introduce her to your old man."

"She is."

"I'm glad to see that therapy finally paid off. Your mother and I never thought we'd see the day that you'd settle down."

"I'm not quite there yet, but I'm working on it."

"Part of Blaise will always be wild. It's in his nature," Mercy snarks.

"How about we let the three of them visit. You can come with me to Thayer's house. I need to make sure her security system is all set up." I glance at my watch.

"Did she have an issue?"

"I'll explain it to you on the ride over."

"Not before I steal a hug from my favorite niece." He scoots past me to Mercy, and I shake Uncle Ethan's hand.

"I'm glad the two of you are here to keep her under control."

He laughs. "That's not likely to happen unless she's strapped to the bed. She's never been one for sitting still. Not even as a kid."

"I'm ready if you are." Dad steps beside me.

"Try to behave," I holler over my shoulder to Mercy, and she flicks me off with a grin. "That's the Mercy I love and adore." I chuckle and head down the stairs with my father behind me.

We drive through town, and I point out Katherine's building and the bakery, promising him we'd stop on the way back to bring home cinnamon rolls. I see Chase outside the sheriff's office and honk the horn, pulling into the parking lot. My father gets out and hugs him.

"It's so good to see you, Chase."

"This is a nice surprise."

"Yeah, I tagged along with Jane and Ethan."

"I'll call Atley and have her change our dinner plans. We'll come over after work."

"Sounds great."

"Where are you two headed?" Chase asks me.

"I'm going to check on Thayer's security system and introduce her to my father."

"Good thing it's being installed. I spoke with the sheriff in Boston. He sent his men to Brent's last known address, and the place was empty, and they were unable to locate him. If he shows up here, I'll be able to arrest him for breaking his probation. I'm on my way to have posters of his face printed and plastered all over this town."

"Do me a favor, and don't tell Thayer he's MIA."

"I'll leave that up to you."

"Are you going to fill me in?" Dad's face grows serious.

"I gotta go. I'll see you at the main house later." Chase taps the roof of my truck.

Dad gets back in the passenger side and buckles. I tell him about Thayer's stalker on the way to her house.

"She must be terrified," he says.

"She puts on a brave face, and she's had to deal with a lot. She thought moving to Montana would keep her safe."

"I'm sure you intend on taking care of her."

"The security system will help."

"I'm surprised you haven't moved her into your room." He chuckles.

"Believe me, it was the first thing out of my mouth, but she wasn't having it. Thayer doesn't want to feel trapped by him, and I can't say that I blame her."

I make the turn to her house and park in her drive-way. "You might want to let me go in first. If she's been in her writing cave, we'll startle her."

"Wait. Did you say her name is Thayer? Your mother has a bookshelf full of paperbacks by a Thayer Hawkins. It couldn't be the same person."

"It is. She writes romance books, and I don't want to think about my mother reading her stories." I laugh.

"I'm going to call Molly and tell her. She'll want to meet her. Perhaps I can bring her home a signed book." He whips out his phone, and I make my way to the door, knocking lightly.

"Hey, babe," I holler. "It's just me."

"I'm in my room!" she yells.

"I thought you might be." I lay a kiss on the top of her head.

"You calling me babe has me hot and bothered."

"You might want to cool your jets. My father is in my truck."

She hops to her feet. "Why didn't you tell me he was coming to town?" She rummages through her drawers to change out of her sweats.

"Because I had no idea he was coming. I have to warn you. When I told him your name, he recognized it from my mother's collection of books. Evidently, she's a fan."

She laughs. "You're totally embarrassed by that."

"No...not embarrassed," I snort. "I just don't want to think about the things my mother has read. Especially if our sexcapades end up in one of your books."

"Oh, you can count on that," she teases me with a quick peck to the cheek.

"I'm ready to meet the man that raised you." She holds out her hand, and I weave my fingers with hers.

We walk outside, and Dad gets out of the truck when he sees us. "Dad, this is Thayer Hawkins. The woman who's stolen my heart." I clutch her to my side.

"It's so nice to meet you." Instead of gripping her hand, he hauls her to his chest. "Welcome to our family."

"Thank you. I see where Blaise gets his good looks from," she grins.

"I give the credit to his mother. Speaking of which, she's dying to meet you." He spins his phone around, and it's on a video call.

"Hi, Mom." I wave, and Dad hands Thayer the phone. She disappears into the house with it.

"She's beautiful, Son."

"I'm afraid I've lost her to my mother. There's no telling how long she'll keep her on that call." I chuckle and usher my father around, checking out the security system.

20

THAYER

"I bet you've loved having your father here the past week." My hands glide over his bare chest as I rub massage oil on him.

"I did, but he was ready to get back home. He should be landing in Kentucky as we speak with Mercy's parents."

"Your dad would get along really well with mine. They seem to be similar-minded on major issues."

"I know he really liked you." He grins, resting one hand behind his head.

"The feeling was very mutual, and if he wasn't a married man..." I tease, and he tickles me. "Alright! Alright!" I howl, needing to catch my breath.

He settles back against the pillow. "My mom and dad are inseparable. I've always admired their marriage, and after all these years, they're still madly in love. Prior to meeting you, I didn't think I'd ever want to be like them."

My hands still on his chest. "You want to get married?"

He clears his throat. "Not today, but someday, maybe not in the not-so-distant future." He drapes a hand around my waist. "What do you think about that?"

"One day, yes."

"Would a city girl like you ever consider marrying a cowboy like me?" A seriousness creases the corners of his eyes.

"I'd marry the man I love whether he was from the city or the country. All I want is someone with a good heart." My hand splays over the left side of his chest.

"He doesn't even have to be good-looking?" He laughs.

"It couldn't hurt." I scrunch my nose.

"You mean to tell me I've been wasting my good looks and charm on you, and all I had to do was be kind?" he roars, and I fall in love with his playful side.

"Your handsome face and sexy body have not been wasted on me in the least. In fact, I think it's done wonders for every inch of my body." I wiggle my ass.

"Keep that up, and we'll go for round three." He lifts his hips.

My phone rings, and I grab it off of the nightstand. "It's a Boston number." The hair on my arms stands up.

Blaise snatches it out of my hand. "Hello!" he barks.

I assume it's silent on the other end when he repeats himself.

"Hello!"

"Hang up," I mouth the words silently.

"Listen here, you sick son of a..." He stops shy of swearing and looks at the phone. "He hung up." His teeth gnash. "Have you heard anything back from Chase?"

I debate telling him. If I don't, he'll only be angrier. "He spoke with his contact in Boston. Brent's place was emptied out, and there's been no sign of him."

I fall over on the bed as he jumps up and snags his phone. "I'm calling the security company!" he snaps and storms out the front door, slamming it.

"What's eating him?" Sage asks when I walk into the kitchen, tying my robe.

"I got another call from that number in Boston, and I told them Brent is missing."

"I don't blame him for being upset then." She pours her milk from her cereal bowl down the sink. "Are both of you coming to the soft opening at Katherine's building tonight? She's showcasing my artwork on every floor."

"We wouldn't miss it for the world. I can't wait until your gallery opening in a few months."

"I've got a lot of work to do before then. I forgot to mention that right after the opening tonight, I'm taking the redeye to the coast of Oregon for a photo shoot with a company that rescues injured seals. I won't be back until next weekend."

"I'm glad things are going so well for you. Are you bringing a date to the opening tonight?"

"I asked Jace to escort me." She lifts one shoulder nonchalantly.

"Is there a spark between the two of you?" I waggle my brows.

"There could be, but we agreed to be just friends. Both of us are too busy to commit to anything else."

"As in friends with benefits?" I grin.

"Strictly platonic. Not that I'd be opposed to a roll in the hay with him, but I don't want the distraction right now."

"I'd hardly call sex with a rugged cowboy a distraction," I hoot.

"I just mean I'd want more, and my career comes first. He's going to be working on becoming a fireman, so he'll be equally as busy. Besides, it might be a little awkward being that he and Blaise are cousins. If I broke his heart, it might cause a rift between me and his family, and I don't want to be on the wrong side of any of the Calhouns."

"They are a loyal bunch. Perhaps you're right. Best to leave well enough alone."

"Agreed. I gotta get out of here. I'll see you this evening."

I walk her to the door so that I can check on Blaise. He's stuffing the phone in his back pocket, stomping toward me while he tilts his hat at Sage.

"Have they seen anything on camera?"

"Nothing, but they'll be more diligent to look for anything out of the ordinary now that they know your routine."

"Sounds like they're the ones stalking me," I mutter.

"We've talked about this at length. It's for your own good and Sage's. Let's go over the silent alarm one more time and where your handgun is kept."

I roll my eyes skyward. "It's really not difficult to push a button. I don't think I need to practice doing it. And my gun is right where you strapped it to the side of my nightstand, and there's one under the table in the kitchen." I prop my hands on my hips.

He lifts his wrist, peering at this watch. "I have to get to work. I wish you'd just give in and come stay at the ranch. It would make things a lot easier."

I weave my hands between his arms and waist, resting them on his lower back. "How about if I agree to come stay with you while Sage is out of town. She leaves tonight after the opening and will be gone until next weekend. Either that, or we could have the place to ourselves so you can do all sorts of naughty things to me." I nip his chin with my teeth.

"As delicious as that sounds, I've been late for work every day since I've been staying here, and if you wouldn't be so noisy, I could still have my way with you in my own bedroom." He slaps my ass, and I squeal.

"Fine. You win, but I'm not the loud one." I peck his cheek and wave at him from the porch as he pulls out of the driveway.

I hurry and get dressed in a pair of skinny jeans and a soft, silky green blouse, pairing it with flats for my shopping spree. I want to get something nice for the opening tonight. I've yet to check out the stores in town, so I'm not sure what I'll find.

I park across from a small clothing boutique that I've walked by several times when I've gone to the brewery. After finding a few dresses, I head to the dressing room and run into Knox outside one of the rooms peering into a full-length mirror, wearing a pale yellow dress with a price tag attached to the sleeve.

"That looks nice on you," I say, and her gaze meets mine in the mirror.

"Oh, hey. You must be doing the same thing—shopping for something to wear to the event tonight. My hubby is adamant that I can't wear blue jeans or anything plaid," she snorts.

"That's funny. Blaise has been trying to get me into plaid."

She turns to face me and goes through the dresses in my hand. "None of these will do." She gnaws at her cheek.

"What's wrong with them? I don't want too fancy. I have those types of clothes in my closet."

"These are fine for an old married woman who doesn't want her husband to know she has tits." She takes them from me and hangs them on the return rack. "Come with me. We're going to find us a sexy dress that will turn our men on the minute they lay eyes on us."

"I could wear a sackcloth, and Blaise would have it on the ground in two seconds flat," I mutter, and she laughs.

"Beck would prefer me to run around naked, but neither one of us would accomplish anything." She tugs my hand, and I follow her through the store. Pushing back a few hangers, she pulls out a dress. "This would look stunning on you."

It's a short, satin, light shade of lavender, off-the-shoulder dress. "It's definitely not plaid."

"The best part is the back." She spins the hanger around, and the back makes a V shape all the way down to the lower part of where it would fit on the hips.

"That's a little sexier than I'd choose for myself."

"Exactly. Try it on." She holds it toward me, then snatches a shimmery gray-colored dress for herself.

"I don't know..."

"Just give it a try. I bet you're going to love it." She yanks my hand, leaving me no choice but to follow her. "I want to see it on you," she quips then closes her curtain.

I glance at the size, and surprisingly, she nailed it. Slipping out of my clothes, I step into the dress and wiggly into it. The material feels amazingly soft, and the fit leaves nothing to the imagination.

"Do you have it on?" Knox peeks through my curtain, and her mouth falls open.

"What? Does it look terrible?"

"You have to see for yourself." She holds the curtain back, and I step out in front of the mirror.

"I have to admit, it does look fantastic on me." I flatten the material over my waist.

"And, girl, wait until you see your backside. Blaise's eyeballs are going to bounce right out of their sockets." She spins me in the mirror, and I turn my head for a look. The dress hugs my hips and sits at the dimples of my lower back. "It's a little short. I can almost see my—"

"Pink canoe." She smiles, and I bust out laughing.

"Not exactly what I was going to say, but I have to admit, I really like it. You don't think it's too much for the opening? All eyes should be on the building, not us." I run my fingertips over the spaghetti strap of her dress. "You look amazing."

"Why can't they be on both? I hardly get a night of fun, and I fully plan on taking advantage of my cowboy...I mean the night." She winks.

"You'd be a great character in one of my books," I snort. "I love your spunk."

"You mean dirty mind." She elbows me.

"That too." I can't help but grin, thinking how much I really like her.

"Let's buy these and find perfectly matching shoes and then go to lunch."

"I'd like that very much."

We change, make our purchase, then hit the shoe store at the end of the block. I settle on a nude color two-inch heel, and Knox finds a pair of black, slinky, four-inch heels.

"These are going to look so yummy around Beck's neck." She dangles them from a finger, and I roar at her antics.

"For some reason, I don't think the two of you need any more spice in your life."

"I wouldn't settle for anything less, and neither should you. Knowing Blaise, it shouldn't be an issue."

"It most definitely is not." I giggle like a schoolgirl.

As we are checking out, Blaise's name flashes on my phone. "Hey," I answer it wearing a cheese-eating grin.

"Hi, gorgeous. I just wanted to tell you that I love you."

My heart melts. "I love you too."

"What are you doing?"

"I've had the best morning shopping with Knox."

"Really? How did that happen, and do I need to rescue you?"

"I ran into her while shopping for a dress for tonight. She helped me find the perfect one."

I can hear him swallow hard. "I'm going to sport a hard-on all night, aren't I?"

"Most assuredly." I bust a gut.

"My mind just wandered to the dark room we set up in Sage's gallery." His tone is full of the lust he's feeling.

"I don't think Sage would appreciate us defiling her dark room." As I envision it, a warmth builds between my thighs with an ache for him.

"Nobody says she has to know about it." He chuckles. "I'll pick you up at seven."

"I'm going to help Sage with some finishing touches at the gallery, so I'll just meet you there."

"Alright. Have fun with Knox, but text me a 911 if you need me to save you."

"I'll be fine," I snort. "I really like her."

"She's good peeps, just with a dirty mind."

"I'm okay with that." He tells me he loves me one more time before he ends our call, and my heart melts with happiness.

21

BLAISE

"You look handsome. I wish I was going tonight to support Kat." Mercy waves me to her bedside to straighten my bolo tie. "It seems like the only time us women get our men out of plaid is weddings and special occasions."

"Yeah, well, I'd have been just as happy in mine had Knox not been busting my chops to look a little nicer." I tug at the collar of my shirt. "She's even got Jace wearing a pair of black slacks. I don't believe I've ever seen him in anything other than Wranglers."

"You'll have to snap some pictures for me."

"Is Hardin staying here with you?"

She sighs. "I tried to convince him to go, but he doesn't trust me to stay in bed."

"I can't say that I blame him," I snort. "How much longer are you on bed rest?"

"Atley will reassess me at my next visit in a week. She thinks I'll be able to not be held captive in my room at that point, but she won't be releasing me for work."

"Are you going to go back to your livestock position once the baby is born?"

"I'm going to shift from fieldwork to working from home."

"Good, because I know once your son is born, you won't want to leave him."

"Baby Ethan." She rubs her belly. "I can't wait until he arrives."

I lean down and kiss her cheek. "Thanks for the help with my bolo."

"Have fun tonight, and give Katherine my love."

"Will do."

Jace is waiting for me on the landing of the stairs. "Everyone else has already left. Can I hitch a ride with you?"

"Sure," I say, and we load up in my truck. "So, you and Sage, huh?"

"We're just friends, and we've agreed to keep it that way."

"Probably a smart decision. You're going to be balls to the walls busy here shortly learning to be a fireman."

"I love ranching, but I'm so excited to be doing something else."

"I know the feeling. Tinkering with engines is what I was meant to do. Ranching is for pure pleasure."

"You seem happy. In fact, happier than I've ever seen you."

"I am, thanks to finding Thayer."

"It's about damn time." He slaps me on the shoulder.

"She came out of nowhere for me, and I fell for her so quickly."

"I think it's a family trait. It's been that way for all the members of our family. When you know...you know, man. No sense wasting your time with anyone else."

He chats about the program he'll be starting until we parallel park in the only spot left on Main Street. "Appears the entire town is coming to the opening of the building tonight."

"Katherine and Walker did a good job getting the word out."

Clicking the button to lock my truck, we make our way to the crosswalk and wait for the signal to turn, along with several couples heading in the same direction. I hold open the glass door for others to go through first, and as soon as my shiny boots hit the tile floor, I'm scanning the room for Thayer. She's handing out fluted glasses of champagne at the makeshift all-brass bar nestled against the back wall. Her face lights up when she sees me with an appreciative wink.

She flips her hair over her shoulder as she saunters toward me, and I'm instantly tight in my pants. One of my favorite places to kiss her is bare. The dip of her collarbones meeting the lavender material has me itching to touch her. Pink lips land gently on my mouth, and I inhale her sweet scent.

"You look beautiful." I choke back a rasp.

"You look pretty handsome yourself, cowboy." She tugs at my bolo.

"Would you like a glass of champagne?"

I nod.

She turns on her heels, and a moan gets lodged in my chest, seeing her backside and my feet forget to move.

When she realizes I'm not behind her, she gazes over her shoulder. "Are you coming?"

"I think I just did." My Adam's apple bobs repeatedly.

Her skin blushes the color of Elvis's famous Cadillac. My sense of self-preservation when it comes to this woman has flown out of control. My need for her is beyond my understanding. I've slept with numerous women, but never have I felt the physical pleasure I do with Thayer. I tried never to take their hearts, but hers I want owned solely by me. My need for her is raw and not something I intended on feeling.

"Fuck the champagne," I mutter under my breath and stomp toward her with purpose, taking her hand and drawing her into the gallery.

"Where are we going?" She can barely keep up.

Searching the space, when no one is looking, I open the door to the dark room, pull the chain on the small hanging light, and haul her inside, shutting it behind us. I don't give her time to speak again before my lips are feverishly crashing on hers.

"Blaise," she moans my name.

My savage hands cup her breast, and my teeth find her collarbone. Any resistance she was giving me melts in my arms.

"You. Are. So. Damn. Irresistible." I'm swimming with so much desire I can hardly stand it. My tongue finds its way up the column of her neck, and my breath explodes close to her ear. "This is going to be quick and hard." Grasping her by the hips, I'm sure they'll be marked up. I spin her around and press the palms of her hands on the wall. "Don't move," I order, then slide one hand underneath her dress, removing the barrier between us while simultaneously unzipping my pants and releasing my engorged cock. Widening her stance, I slide my fingers through her folds, finding she's as turned on as I am. I take one step back to admire her spine and kiss her from the back of her neck to the dip of the material above her ass.

"I thought you said this was going to be quick?" She's all breathy.

"I had to take a minute to enjoy what turned me on so much." In one deep thrust, I'm buried inside of her, and she gasps, clutching her fingertips into the wall. Slamming into her, reaching her deepest parts, she tightens around me. My desire rages in my veins, and I reach around and rub her numb, and there's no stopping her orgasm.

She breathes my name like a prayer. "Blaise."

I answer her by filling her repeatedly through her orgasm with a fierceness behind every thrust. "I'm going to come," I roar. My body buzzes for release, and I'm damn sure not going to hold anything back. Burying myself inside of her one more time, a desperate moan passes my lips, and I still deep within her, physically satiated.

Her breath is as ragged as mine as she turns to face me with my hands planted where hers left. "I can't believe we just did that."

"I'm sorry, but you left me no choice when I saw you in that dress. You're going to have to remove it, or I'm going to be insanely jealous of any man that looks at you."

"I can't walk around naked." She laughs. "You're just going to have to learn self-control. Besides, what we just did should've gotten it out of your system."

"Not even close." I swallow, trying to tamper down the dryness of my throat.

She shimmies her panties over her hips. "We've got to get back out there before the tour starts. Sage will want to share her dark room."

Reluctantly, I zip my pants. She cracks open the door and peeks outside. "This place is booming with people. I'll go first." She steps out and shuts the door.

Giving her a minute, I follow suit. She's already back at the bar with her dress perfectly in place, but the skin on her shoulders shows evidence of where I've been. Smiling with pride, I mingle among the guests while watching her out of the corner of my eye.

Knox hands me a drink. "That didn't take you very long," she snorts.

"What are you talking about?"

She adjusts my collar. "I told her that dress would drive you wild. We didn't even make it inside the building before Beck took what he wanted from me."

"That dress is amazing, but it's the woman inside it, that does it for me."

"Yeah, but the dress is what will keep you wild." She playfully smacks her palm to my cheek. "And that is what women love."

Thayer sashays next to Knox and bumps her with her hip. "You're a bad influence on him. Keep it up." She giggles.

Sage walks between us. "By the color pink on your skin, I can only assume you two christened this place. I don't even want to know where, but try to behave yourselves for the rest of the evening."

We all burst out in laughter. Sage takes Thayer's hand to start the tour of the gallery while Kat and Walker speak to the crowd of people, welcoming them and giving the history of the building and its purpose now.

Jace and I make our way upstairs, and I notice several guests stop to admire Sage's prints show-cased on the walls.

"She's a really good photographer," Jace states. "These are all for sale in her gallery on the first floor," he tells them.

"Friends, huh?" I nudge him with my elbow.

"Friends help friends," he shrugs.

"True," I chuckle. We continue to roam the open floor plan with different types of offices behind glass walls. On the second floor, there are realtor's offices and a web designer. The third floor boasts a hair salon and a massage parlor, along with a baby boutique and a jewelry store.

We make our way back downstairs to the back of the building, where there is a large kitchen with multiple ovens and kitchen appliances on the counters with several working stations in the middle. I listen as Kat starts speaking over the crowd.

"This area has several purposes. It can be used when someone needs to cater a large event, and they need the space to assemble, or cooking classes will be held here. You can register online for the classes and schedule a time to reserve the kitchen for whatever your needs may be."

"Your wife really has gone all out." I clasp Walker on the shoulder.

"She's an amazing businesswoman." He beams with pride.

"This place is going to be busy."

"She's already rented every office space and has a waiting list."

"Good thing Thayer moved quickly to get Sage the gallery in here. She's going to be a huge success."

We stand shoulder to shoulder as Kat continues to speak to the guests. I sweep the room, hoping to lay my eyes on Thayer but don't see her.

"Excuse me. I need to go find Thayer," I tell him and make my way through the crowd of people to the front. Sage is in the gallery behind the counter ringing up a customer that bought one of her photos of a bald eagle.

I wait off to the side until she's done. "Have you seen Thayer?"

"Not recently. She said she was going to find you. I thought she'd be back by now."

"Hmmm," I grunt. "Perhaps she's on another floor." I move through the people on the stairs and search the second floor, then the third. A jolt of fear rests on the back of my neck when I can't find her. Trudging down the stairs, I return to the gallery.

"I can't find her," I tell Sage, rubbing my neck.

"I'm sure she's somewhere. She wouldn't leave without saying something. She promised to stay and lock up the gallery so that I don't miss my flight."

Digging my phone free of my back pocket, I dial her number and hear her phone ringing. Sage leans down and picks up Thayer's purse from underneath the counter.

"See, she's still in the building somewhere. She can't go anywhere without her keys."

My gut is telling me something's not right, but I try to listen to her voice of reason. "I'm going to go look for her again. If she shows up here, tell her to stay put."

She salutes me.

Retracing my steps, there's still no sign of her. I run into Jace coming out of the men's restroom. "Have you seen Thayer?"

"Yeah, about fifteen minutes ago. She said she had a severe headache, and she was going home to lie down for a bit."

My chest frantically thuds. "Was there anyone with her?"

"There was a man a few feet behind her, but I wouldn't necessarily say he was with her."

Chase walks toward the bathroom, and I stop him. "Do you have a picture of Brent on your phone," I ask him, feeling a deep desperation.

"Yeah. I kept the photo I sent out to my men. Why?" He scowls.

"Show Jace," I bark.

He flips through files on his phone and opens one of them, then turns the picture toward Jace.

"Is that the man you saw?" I ask.

He squints. "He had a beard, but those eyes are the same."

"Shit!" I grit out.

"You saw this man in town?" Chase asks.

"He was here at the gallery standing behind Thayer."

"Are you one hundred and ten percent sure this is the man you saw?"

Jace takes a closer look. "I'm positive. He was standing right there." He points.

I call the security company, and they tell me they had been trying to get ahold of Thayer to let her know they saw a man approaching her house on the security camera, but she never answered.

"Why the hell didn't you call me?" I howl. I change to speakerphone so Chase can listen.

"We did. We left you a voicemail." I look at my phone and see the notification in the corner alerting me of a message. "I didn't hear it ring."

"We dispatched the police to her place because when we called the sheriff's office, they said he was off duty tonight."

Chase whips out his phone and steps away.

"How long ago was the man seen at her place?"

"An hour and fifteen minutes ago, to be exact."

I hang up when Chase ambles back over. "I spoke to the cop that was dispatched to her place. There was no sign of a break-in, so they chalked it up to nothing."

"I've got to find her," I growl, flooded with fear.

22

THAYER

As much as I try to focus on helping Sage, my gaze voluntarily keeps gliding over to her dark room. I can still feel Blaise's strong hands holding my hips in place as he thrust in and out of me from behind. It's not just sex, even though that's far more amazing than I ever thought possible. It's the way he looks at me, speaks to me...his eyes filled with so much love, more than I'd ever imagine finding. My heart is bursting to be with him, and my body is in overdrive, needing to be near him.

"Hey, do you mind if I sneak away for a minute or two to find Blaise?" I ask Sage.

"You just can't get enough of him, can you?" she howls.

"Is that a bad thing?"

"Not at all." She squeezes my arm.

"He's utterly taken me off guard, and I'm finding it hard to breathe without him near me."

"You've got it bad," she snorts. "Go. I can handle this until you come back."

"Thanks," I say, skating off to find him. I search the second floor, and I see two women standing in the corner, whispering, and pointing at Blaise. He's clueless to either one of them. One smiles and licks her pouty lips, and the other one can't take her gaze from his ass.

"I'm going to put a stop to this," I rant to myself and march over to them. "You can quit eye-fucking him any day now. He's off the market."

"And I suppose you're the one who took him off?" Her gaze rakes down my body.

"I am." I stick my chin in the air.

"I don't mind sharing him in bed if you don't," the other one purrs. "I can do a trio or more." She lifts a sultry shoulder.

"He's not a bargaining chip, and neither am I. Back off and leave him alone," I grit out between my teeth while keeping my voice low so as not to cause a scene.

One of them flips her hair over her shoulder and moves on to another man. The other hand touches my arm when I go to leave. "You're lucky. He's a good man. You must be something really special because I tried like hell to get to that closed-up heart of his. I'm not sure what you had to offer him that I didn't, but good luck." She saunters off to her friend.

When I turn around, Blaise is no longer there. "I'll find him after I pee." I hustle to the first floor, ready to burst.

Washing my hands, I can still see the pink tinges on the sensitive skin on my neck where Blaise was pecking. That now familiar heat that fills me every time I think about him has saturated me, and I recall our conversation about marriage. Yes, I'd marry him in a heartbeat. I don't care that we haven't known each other very long. In my heart, I know there is no other man for me, so why waste time. I want a full-fledged life with him with lots of babies.

"I'm going to tell him," I mutter and press my lips together, building up my courage. With my feet aimed to find him, when I walk out of the bathroom, a man's large hand snags my arm, and for a brief moment, I think it's something Blaise would do. Ambush me to find another place to screw my brains out.

A voice whispers in my ear, and I'm instantly terrified. Brent.

"Don't say a word or try to get away from me. If you do, I'll open fire in this place." He digs something hard into my back, which I can only assume is a gun. "Do we have an understanding?"

I slowly nod.

"If someone stops us on the way out, make up an accuse, or I'll kill whoever it is speaking to you."

He places his hand on the middle of my back on my bare skin and bile rises in my throat as he strokes my spine and then urges me to walk.

As we round the corner, I see Jace coming my way. "What a great turnout." He smiles.

"Yes, so much more than I expected." I force the corners of my lips to raise.

"I think Sage could use our help. I'll escort you through the crowd." He extends his elbow.

"I have a killer headache, and I'm going to go home and lie down to see if I can knock it out." I press my fingertips into my temples.

"Oh, alright. Do you need a ride?"

"No, I'm good. Thanks." I brush past him before he digs further with questions or gets suspicious.

"Good girl," Brent says once I clear the door. "I'm parked in the alley near the back." He keeps his hand on my shoulder as we walk. "Did you really think I was going to let you move on to someone else?"

"I'm not seeing anyone," I lie to protect Blaise.

"You smell of cologne, and you expect me to believe you?" he huffs, shoving me toward his car. "I told you if I couldn't have you, no one else would either.

Seems you need to be reminded of such." He unlocks the door and shoves me into the passenger side. When he walks around the vehicle, I try to escape, but the door won't open.

My body trembles in fear. "Please don't do this," I beg as he starts the engine.

"Too late for begging." He squeals out of the alley.

"Where are you taking me?" Tears stream down my face.

"Somewhere we can be alone, and if you put up a fight, you'll leave me no choice other than to kill you." He cuts his gaze to me. "It's not what I want to do. If you'd just agree to be with me, there'd be no struggle."

My defiant mind overheats. "I want nothing to do with you!" I scream.

"Aw, you don't mean that, Pumpkin. What we once had was the best. We can get there again." He touches my arm, and I jerk out of his reach.

"We had nothing!"

"You loved me."

"I hate you!"

"You know what they say, there's a fine line between love and hate."

"There is no line! I undoubtedly hate you!"

"You'll change your mind or else." He drums his fingers on the steering wheel. "Is it the man I saw sneak out behind you in the dark room, which I helped myself to a tour of when he got out. It's the hint of his cologne I smell."

He was watching me? How did I not see him? Because I was too engrossed in Blaise. Other than the dark beard, he looks the same. He should've stood out like a sore thumb, but I let my guard down, and now here I am in his clasp again. I've got to find a way to get free of him and contact Blaise. *My phone.* I left it in my purse in the gallery, along with my gun tucked inside.

Swiping away my tears with the back of my hand, I focus on the road and where we are going.

"That dress looks good on you. You never wore anything like that for me."

The look he's giving me is disgusting. What did I ever see in this man? He was charming and knew all the right things to say and do until he didn't. When I started getting glimpses of things I didn't like about him, he turned the tables, and his pure evil was let loose.

"Shit," he snaps. "We've got to stop and get fuel if we're going to make it to our destination."

"Where is that exactly?" My lip quivers.

"We're going primitive for the night. I hate camping, but I didn't want to rent a hotel room to leave a trail."

"Are we staying in a campground?"

"Ha, no way. I found a remote spot with one of those fancy yurts on a mountain about twenty-five miles east of here. We'll be able to get reacquainted without anyone bothering us."

"You've been planning this."

"I've been staking out the little town you've been held up in for a week. I saw you and your friend leaving the gallery one day, and when I read the announcement about the opening, I assumed you'd be there, and I was right."

"I'm begging you, don't do this." I try the door again.

"I fixed it so you can't open it from the inside, so settle down," he snarls.

He turns off his bright lights when he pulls up to a gas pump at a convenience store. "Don't try anything," he warns.

"I didn't get the chance to eat all day. I'm starving." If he lets me go in the store, I'll find a way to leave a trail if I can't escape him.

"Fine. I'll take you inside once I fuel up." He slams the door and keeps his stare on me. I want to search the car for anything I can use for a weapon, but he's watching me.

I've got to come up with a plan, or he's going to kill me because I'll never give him what he wants.

The pump stops, and he opens my door. "Don't try anything foolish. The same thing applies. If you try to escape, I'll start shooting, and whoever dies will be your fault." He flashes his gun tucked beneath his jacket.

I get out and smooth down my dress and scan the area as we walk. There are four cars parked and a lone trucker fueling up. I can't be responsible for their lives, so screaming for help isn't an answer. Once inside, I walk down the chip aisle and tuck a bag under my arm, and make my way to the drink station. To the left of me, there's an aisle with a few makeup items, and it gives me an idea, thanks to Blaise. When Brent looks away at the sound of the door jingling as it opens, I snatch a tube of lipstick and stuff it between my breasts, then proceed to the soda fountain. When we're in line, I rock back and forth on my feet.

"I really have to pee," I tell him.

"You went before we left," he says out of the corner of his mouth.

"I drank too much champagne."

He growls under his breath, and once he's paid cash for the fuel and my food items, he walks with me over to the restroom and pushes open the women's bathroom door, and glances inside. "There's nowhere for you to run. You have precisely two minutes to do your business before I come in after you." He takes the chips and drink from my hands.

I nod and walk inside, and wait until the door closes. Frantically, with my hands shaking, I peel open the lipstick and write a message on the mirror. Waving my hand beneath the faucet, the water turns on, and I make sure to remove any trace of the lipstick and toss the tube in the trash can just as the door swings open with Brent's shoulder shoving it. I rush over before he can stick his head inside.

"All done," I say, and don't slow my pace.

He hesitates like he's debating going into the bathroom but shuts the door and hustles to catch up with me, and I breathe a silent breath of relief.

23

BLAISE

"I sent out an APB to my men. With the timeline Jace provided, it's too late to cut off traffic leaving town. If he's driven from Boston, my men will be on alert for his license plate number." Chase looks as frustrated as I feel, running his hand through his beard.

"And, if he didn't?" I raise the question.

"My men are searching the database for recent car rentals."

"He had to have been scoping out the place. He wouldn't have known she'd be here unless he's been tailing her."

"True. I'll have my men pull up video surveillance footage of Main Street to include a couple weeks back."

"If he knew she was here, why did he go to her place?"

"The report came back with no visible sign of a break-in. That doesn't mean he didn't enter her house," Chase reads the report.

"Then he was looking for something specific."

"Stalkers often want to collect a physical item to retain like a trophy, but finding out what he took is not going to help us find her. Did Thayer drive herself tonight?"

"Thayer's car," I say, and we scramble to get outside only to find it where I saw it parked when I arrived.

"I'll have it dusted for fingerprints," Chase states as he walks around the vehicle, careful not to touch it.

"Thayer!" My gut-wrenching scream bellows down the street, echoing in the night air.

Chase walks to the back of the car and stares. "I want to take a look inside the trunk."

"You think she's inside?" I choke out.

"I don't know, but I'm damn sure going to look."

"Her keys are in the gallery," I tell him, pointing in the direction of the building.

"I'll go get them," Jace starts to run.

"They are in her purse under the counter!" I holler.

Chase paces keeping one hand inside his jacket where he carries a gun in his holster.

"She can't be in the trunk. He wanted her alive. Why would he stuff her in there?" My voice cracks, and my heart is pounding in my ears.

"If she put up a fight—"

"I got the keys!" Jace bellows, gasping for air, tossing them to Chase.

He presses the button, and I hold my breath, praying like hell she's not in there.

Chase shines his flashlight inside the empty trunk. "Thank God," he exhales. As he's closing it, my phone chirps, and I snatch it from my pocket and see an unknown number.

"Answer it," Chase orders, and I put it on speakerphone.

"Thayer." I hope like hell it's her.

"I'm calling this number because I found it written on a mirror at a gas station."

"Where?" Chase takes over.

"Five miles outside of Missoula, headed east at the Gas Depot. There was more to the message," the female caller says. "It was hard to read because it looked pretty shaky, but I believe it said yurt in a mountain."

"Yurt in a mountain?" I repeat.

"I hope you find whoever wrote this." She hangs up.

"Wait!" I yell into my phone.

Chase is already talking to someone on his radio.

"I know where that store is." I grind my teeth.

"Get in my truck," Chase growls, and the three of us take off for it as Sage runs out of the building.

"What's going on? Did you find her?"

"That savage took her," I bark, "and I'm going to find her. Go back inside."

"I'm going with you!"

"Like you hell you are. I'm not risking your life." I get nose-to-nose with her, and Chase intervenes.

"Just let us handle it. Thayer would not want you to put your life in danger."

"You sure as hell better call me the minute you lay eyes on her," she seethes, "and you need to hurry because he'll kill her if she doesn't concede to what he wants."

"We'll find her," I say, then get in Chase's truck.

He talks on his radio as he races with his lights on through town, headed to the gas station. "I've got my men working on locating any yurts within a fifty-mile radius."

The fifteen-minute drive is shortened to ten minutes with Chase speeding, but it seemed like a lifetime. The three of us jump out and race inside and look for the restroom sign. Chase flashes his credentials, and we run to the back and swing open the ladies' room door to find a worker leaning toward the mirror with a rag to clean it.

"Stop!" I yell, holding out my hands, and it frightens the lady.

Chase steps up. "It's okay." He shows her his badge. "That's evidence of a kidnapping." He points.

I square myself in front of the mirror, and my heart thuds seeing her shaky handwriting. "She must be terrified." I read it. "Please help me. Call," and it gives my number, "yurt in mountains, twenty miles east of here."

"Smart girl," Chase states. That will narrow down our search. I don't know how she got him to tell her where he was going, but it's going to save her life." He calls his contact as we get back in his truck and heads east. Within minutes, he has a map of the only mountain twenty minutes from here that has remote camping. "This has to be it." He indicates the red mark on the map.

"He should've never been able to get his hands on her in the first place. This is all my fault." Anger surges in my veins like an angry lion protecting its family.

"You can't take this on yourself. Short of holding her captive, you couldn't keep an eye on her twenty-four seven," Jace says, gripping my shoulder from the back seat.

"That's exactly what I should've been doing rather than drooling all over her. I should've kept myself stationed at the front door and monitored everyone coming inside the building."

"You had no idea he'd show up at such a public event. It was pretty brazen on his part," Chase steps harder on the gas pedal.

"I'll never forgive myself if something happens to her." Tears mixed with rage lodge in my chest.

"She's a smart woman, and she's given us the lead we need to find her. She'll do whatever it takes to stay alive until we can save her from him."

My stomach rolls with pure acid churning. "If he so much as touches her, I'm going to kill him with my bare hands."

The dark road, other than the rotating blue lights, is chilling. It's the same darkness I feel when I retreat inside of myself. Despite my anger, I find my mind dipping into those murky waters with flashbacks of finding Rachel hanging lifelessly and feeling helpless. Squeezing my eyes closed, it's Thayer's pale face that replaces Rachel's as her body swings from the rope. Her name releases with horror-filled fear like I've never known as I try desperately to get her down. When the last fray of the rope is cut, she falls in my arms like a rag doll. Loosening the rope from around her neck, I breathe for her and cry out in pain.

"I can't lose her!" I scream, slamming my fists on the console. "Not again! I'd rather die than see her dead!"

Chase swerves the truck when he takes one hand off of the wheel and grips my forearm. "It's not the same, Blaise. She's not Rachel."

"Don't let yourself go there." Jace is leaning over the seat with his hands on my back.

"We're going to find her," Chase adds. "You have to believe that."

"But what if it's too late?" Tears cloud my eyes, and I lay my forehead on the console and sob.

"I know this is your worst nightmare, but you have to focus on what we know. He doesn't want to kill. In the mind of a stalker, they think of their prey as a possession, so the odds are in our favor that he won't harm her unless she defies him. She's already proven to outsmart him. Having been through this with him before, she knows him and what his limits are. Thayer will use her head and outthink him until we can get to her."

"You're right." I wipe the snot from my face with my sleeve. "She knows him better than anyone."

"That simple fact is what is going to save her life," Chase places his hand back on the steering wheel and focuses on the road, slowing only when we reach the place the map is veering us to turn. His tires land hard on the rocky, narrow road winding up the mountain. He stops and reviews the GPS readings.

"I'm going to drive to this point, and then we'll have to hike the rest. I don't want him to hear or see us coming. We need the element of surprise." He peers in the rearview mirror at Jace. "Under the seat, you'll find a locked box with several guns and ammunition. The key is in the glove box." He indicates with a nod.

I find the key and give it to Jace, who unlocks it and loads the clip in a gun, and hands it to me.

"Be ready for a gunfight," Chase's voice deepens, swarming with concern. "No one dies tonight. You got that?"

I try not to let my fear overwhelm me and focus on every detail of where the headlights hit the darkness for any place I can escape and hide from him until Blaise can find me. *I know he will.*

It's hard to make anything out through all the trees and bumps in the road. We're driving up the side of a mountain that narrows along every curve, and there's no sign of anyone else so far.

"Not much further," he says as if that's supposed to comfort me. It will be the start of my real terror when he stops.

His lights briefly flash on a blue pickup truck parked beside a yurt before we hit another curve in the road. I start counting, making a mental note of how far we travel from it.

"This is the perfect place for us to spend the night and get to know one another again." His gaze skates over me, sending a chill down my spine.

I don't give him the satisfaction of a response.

"What's the matter? The cat got your tongue?"

I swallow hard, still counting.

He reaches over and tucks a tendril of hair behind my ear. "You'll give into me or else."

"Or else what?" I snap my head in his direction. "You'll kill me? Then go ahead. I'd rather die than give you what you want. Besides, if you take my life, you lose me anyway."

"If you force my hand, I will kill you, then I'm going to go hunt down the cowboy with the fancy cologne, and it won't be an easy death. He's responsible for taking you from me."

"I told you I wasn't seeing anyone. What you observed was a onetime fling. Nothing more." I'm a terrible liar, but I have to convince him, so I bite my trembling lip. "I left Boston because of you, not to run into someone else's arms."

"I don't believe you." He makes a hard turn to the left, and I catch myself before I fall into him. "You were never the one-night stand kind of woman." He taps his temple. "You forgot I know you, and I've studied you well."

"People change. I've changed. You did that to me, making me not trust my judgment."

"Then why can't you give me the benefit of the doubt that I've changed too?"

"Because you've kidnapped me!"

"It's for your own good. Nobody is going to love you like I do."

"You don't love me. You only want to possess me!"

I fall forward when he steps on the brakes, planting both of my hands on the dash.

"We're here." He shoves the car into park.

He takes out his gun. "I'm going to go inside and turn on a kerosine lamp. You stay put and don't try to run." He gets out and aims his gun at me through the window.

He disappears into the yurt, and I slide to the driver's side and push open the door and stumble before I get my footing. A sharp pain rips through my hair when I start to run. He grips a handful and twists, yanking me to the ground.

"I told you not to try anything! Now you've forced me to do something I didn't want to do, but being a Boy Scout, I came prepared." He sets the gun in the dirt a few feet away from me, then digs one hand in his pocket while he keeps a firm grip on my hair.

"Hold out your wrists." He grinds his teeth.

My breath quivers, and my hands shake as I take them away from my burning scalp. When he releases my hair, I hold back a sob as my head falls to the ground. Yanking my arms together, he zip-ties my wrists. "You'll have to earn your freedom," he snarls, tucking his hands underneath my shoulders and hauling me to my feet.

Gut-wrenching fear fills me at the thought of what I'll have to do to get him to take these binds off me. At least my feet are free...for now.

Picking up his gun, he drags me by one arm into the yurt. For being buried in a mountain, it's nice, with a full-size bed, a small table, pictures hanging, and fresh-cut flowers all around. An old-fashioned-looking pump for water protrudes through the canvas, and there's a larger cooler sitting next to it.

"I had these flowers delivered just for you," he says with a sickening grin. "There's champagne to celebrate our night together." He pulls me to the bed. "Sit," he commands. "I'll open the bottle. Are you hungry? I have some sandwiches."

"No. How long have you been stalking me?"

"I wouldn't call it stalking. More like keeping an eye out on what's mine." He pops the cork, and the bottle sprays to the ground.

How did I not see him? I was busy trying to live my life and be happy. Now, I've dragged Blaise into my nightmare.

"Here," he says, handing me a glass.

I lift my hands and take it from him, contemplating tossing it in his face, but it will only make matters worse. I need to outthink him. "Thank you." I steady my voice.

"That's more like it." He tips his glass to mine, clinking it. "Here's to a new start for us. I promise I'm going to take good care of you."

I pretend to sip the champagne.

His gaze focuses on my lips. "You're so damn beautiful," he rasps. "I knew the day I met you at your book signing I'd make you mine."

"You won me over with your kindness," I say softly when all I want to do is break this glass and stab him with it.

"I'm still that man, and we can have it all." His fingertips grazing the length of my arm has me wanting to vomit, making my skin crawl.

"Let me love you," he says, kissing my cheek, and I shiver. "Are you cold?"

I nod.

"Don't move a muscle." He points at my face, then ducks out of the tent.

My gaze sweeps the room, looking for anything I can use as a weapon. Scrambling to the cooler, I lift the lid. There's a butter knife inside. I grasp it and tuck it into the side of my underwear at the hip, then hurry back to where he left me just in time for him to throw back the flap of the yurt. He's carrying a black duffel bag.

"I brought you something I knew you wouldn't want to leave behind." He sets it on the bed and unzips it, and I see clothes from my dresser drawer. I gasp when he finds what he's looking for. "I know how special this is to you." He drapes it over my shoulders.

The blanket my mother made for me. "You were in my house?" Horror fills me.

"It was so easy to get in your bedroom window. I waited until you left for the shindig. The way you were dressed, you'd need some clothes for where we are going, and when I saw this folded on your bed, I had to take it. It smells of you," he says at the bridge of my ear and inhales.

I close my eyes as bile rises in my throat.

"Take off your clothes," he orders, stepping away from me. "It's time for bed, and you need to get out of your dress."

"I can't do anything with my hands tied." I turn my back to him. I'll have to let him touch me if I'm going to escape.

"I'll gladly undress you, but I'm not removing your binds." I hear him set his glass down, and I lean down, setting mine on the blue throw rug at the foot of the bed.

He slips his hand to the middle of my back and trails his fingers to the hem of my dress. Slowly, I take the butter knife from my hip when his mouth eases to between my shoulder blades.

I keep it low to my waist, and I fake a pleasurable moan.

"That's my girl. I knew you'd want me," he says and turns me toward him. I sweep the knife upward and jab it into his shoulder. It pierces his skin enough to make him take a step back, and I run, hearing him scream my name.

Branches scratch my skin as I run as fast as I can into the trees. It's pitch black, and I can't see anything. Resting against a tree, I break the zip tie against my shin like my father taught me to do and rub my wrists.

"You can't go very far in the dark!" Brent is scanning the area with a flashlight. "You might as well come back because I'm going to find you."

I'd rather get mauled by a bear than let him get his hands on me again.

"Come on, Thayer. I can forgive you for your bad behavior if you show your face," he yells.

I press flat against the tree when his light shines in my direction.

"I'll give you until the count of ten. If you come out, I promise I won't hurt you. If you don't, then they'll be a consequence to pay when I find you...and I will find you."

His light moves in another direction, and I hold my breath, not wanting to let out a single sound. I peek from behind the tree and see him walking in the opposite direction. Peeling out of my shoes, I ease my steps as carefully and as quietly as I can, following the path of the road down the mountain. I make it a few hundred feet, but I twist my ankle, tripping over a root. I hold in my cry, but I can't bury the sound of me hitting the ground.

His flashlight sweeps down the path I'm on. "There you are," he hollers, taking off in a run.

Clambering to my feet, I limp down the road and see a light coming from the yurt the truck was parked beside. "Help me," I cry, shuffling through the flap.

A shirtless man wearing pajama bottoms gets to his feet.

"Please help me. There's a man coming after me with a gun."

I hide behind him as he reaches for a shotgun resting against the center pole holding up the yurt.

"There's an opening in the back." He hands me a flashlight. "Go. I'll take care of him."

I find the flap, hobble out, and don't look back. My ankle throbs with every step, but I swallow the pain. I don't make it very far when I hear gunfire. I go to my knees and cover my ears, saying a prayer that he got him. My chest heaves faster when I hear my name being screamed into the darkness.

"Thayer! You forced me to kill him! He's dead because of your disobedience!"

"No, no, no!" I wail, getting to my feet.

When he sees me, he sends a single shot into the air. "Don't make me kill you too. I told you what I'd do to that cowboy of yours." Hate fills every fine line of his face, and spit flies from his mouth like a rabid squirrel.

I freeze, knowing he means it. His light shines directly into my face, and I cover my eyes. "I will not hesitate to kill you this time if you try to get away from me." He snatches the flashlight from my hand, and I see blood dripping down his arm.

"The son of a bitch thought he could kill me," he seethes. "Get your sweet ass back up the mountain." His fingernails dig into my forearm as he drags me. I limp behind him. "Serves you right for thinking you could get away."

I feel the warmth of his blood on my skin and know it's only a matter of time before it stops him. When we make it back to the yurt, he shoves me hard, and the bed breaks my fall. I roll over to face him, and he's leaning over with his hands braced on his knees with his gun still in one hand. He lifts it, pointing it at me. "There's a first aid kit under the bed. Get it out."

Crawling to the ground, I reach under the bed and drag out a plastic box. "You really were a Boy Scout, weren't you?"

"I had a feeling you'd cause me trouble." His face is pale, and he's covered in sweat as blood pools on the rug. He sits, aiming his gun at me and holding pressure on his left upper chest with his other hand. "There's gauze and alcohol. I need you to stop the bleeding and clean it out."

"You need to go to the hospital," I say, opening the box and digging through it.

"That's not an option. Hurry up," he sniffs.

Unbuttoning his shirt, I see the gaping hole where the bullet lodged. I stand and look over his shoulder to see if there's an exit wound. "The bullet didn't come out," I tell him.

"Then I guess you'll have to dig it out."

Unscrewing the bottle of alcohol. "You might want to lay down."

"Just fucking do it," he grits out.

Tipping the bottle to his skin, it pours out, and he screams in pain. I shove him back and spin around, running and hearing his gun go off.

25

BLAISE

We're locked and loaded with guns and flashlights, trudging up the mountain.

"Stay wide and keep your eyes peeled," Chase orders, and we spread out on the road.

"According to my GPS signal, we should come upon a campsite around this corner." I aim the beam of the flashlight down the road.

Picking up our pace, we reach it in no time. There's a blue truck parked outside and a dim light flickering inside.

"You go around back," Chase tells Jace and waves me over to him. "This may not be his," he says, inching back the flap to peek inside. "Damn it," he snarls and rushes in, and I follow him.

There's a man crumbled on the floor with a gunshot wound to the gut. "Is he still alive?" I ask Chase, who's squatting next to him.

"He's still breathing."

The man's eyes blink open. "You have to find her," he rasps.

"Find who?" I rush beside him.

"I'm calling for an ambulance." Chase clutches his phone. "Get pressure on his gut," he orders, and I rip off my shirt, pressing it to his gut, and he cries out in pain. "Find who?" I ask again.

"A woman ran into my tent and said she'd been kidnapped."

"Thayer." I cut my gaze to Jace, who came barreling into the yurt.

"There's a blood trail outside," he says solemnly with a horrified look in his eyes.

"I sent her out the back, and he got the better of me, but I think I hit him."

Chase hangs up the phone. "Jace, come take over. The ambulance is on its way. You and I are going after her," he barks. "Don't let off pressure until the paramedics arrive." He and Jace swap spots.

"Thank you for helping her," I tell the man, then hustle out with Chase. He shines his flashlight in the dirt. "Here's the blood trail. It leads up the mountain."

We take off in a full run uphill and around a sharp curve and don't stop until we see another yurt. Chase leverages his weapon in both hands. "This is it," he whispers. "I'll go high, you go low."

We move at the same time when he whips back the opening of the tent. Brent is lying on the bed with his feet still on the floor, and a gun is in his open palm.

"Don't move an inch," Chase growls.

We weave toward him cautiously, and his eyes are closed. I reach out and pick up his gun.

"As much as I want him dead, I hope he's alive so we can find Thayer."

Chase presses two fingers into the side of his neck. "He's alive."

Tucking his gun into my belt and shoving mine in my boot, I lean over him, placing my hands on his throat. "Wake up, you bastard," I shout.

His eyes flutter open, and a sick smile covers his face. "You're too late," he utters.

"Where the hell is she?" Chase presses his gun to Brent's forehead.

"Probably being eaten by a wild cat." He laughs.

I claw my fingers into his throat. "Tell me where the hell she is!"

He gasps for air and pulls at my hands, trying to free himself.

"Tell him, or I'm going to let him draw the last breath out of you." Chase stands tall, watching.

"She ran into the woods." He gulps.

"Was she injured?" Chase asks.

"I shot her," he wheezes, and I squeeze tighter with every intention of killing him.

Chase lays his hand firmly on my shoulder. "That's enough. He'll pay the price for what he's done. If you kill him, he wins."

I struggle to let go. He rolls to his side, heaving for air.

Shining my light on the ground, I aim it toward the door. "All of this blood isn't his." I move toward the flap. "It looks like she was right about here when he shot her." My heart races, needing to find her.

"I'll call for a search party," Chase says as Brent screams out when Chase flips him over to handcuff him.

"There's no time. I'm going out there to find her."

"Then this son of a bitch is coming with us." Brent yells again when Chase hauls him to his feet.

He calls Jace when we hear the ambulance coming up the mountainside. "As soon as the paramedics arrive, come straight up the mountain and follow the curve. You'll see a yurt. I have Brent in handcuffs, and we're headed out to find Thayer. He says he shot her. We could use your help to find her." He hangs up and shoves his gun into Brent's back. "Walk," he growls.

We set out into the trees following her footprints, and when we lose them, we search for drops of blood and broken twigs on bushes.

"She made it pretty far in," Chase states.

"That doesn't mean she ain't dead." Brent chuckles, and I turn around and punch him square in the nose, and he falls to the ground.

"You're just going to let him assault me!" He has the nerve to scream at Chase, rolling around on the ground.

The phone on Chase's hip lights up. "It's Jace," he says, answering it.

"I found her," he says. "I saw where you were headed, and I spanned out to your west."

"Shoot your weapon," Chase tells him.

"Is she alive?" I ask, afraid of the answer.

Gunfire shatters the deafening silence, and we bolt in the direction of the sound, flying over roots and rocks in our path. When I see Jace, I run toward him, and he holds me in his arms.

"Don't." His eyes are filled with fear.

I shove past him and see Thayer lying lifeless against a downed tree with bloody leaves scattered around her.

"No!" My horrifying cry can be heard for miles. I bend down, cradling her in my arms, and I feel for a pulse. "She's still alive." All the air leaves my lungs.

Chase tosses Brent to Jace, who slams him against a tree.

Chase grabs her wrist. "Her pulse is thready, and she's lost a lot of blood. We have to get her off this mountain."

Folding her in my arms, I get to my feet. "I'll carry her," I sniffle and grind my teeth.

Chase calls for another ambulance and backup as we trudge our way down the mountain. I stop suddenly when I hear Thayer whimper.

"Blaise."

"I've got you," I say, kissing her forehead.

"He shot me in the back." She winces.

"I know, baby. You're going to be alright," I assure her, and her head falls back. "Damn it!" I groan and move faster.

As we make it back to the yurt, I can hear the ambulance in the distance. Laying her on the bed, I feel for a pulse again.

"You can't die on me!" I holler and place my hands in the middle of her chest and start compressions. I don't stop until the paramedics arrive and take over, hooking her up to their machines. I stand back, holding my breath and waiting for a blip on the screen to show her heartbeat. There is none. One of them continues thrusting on her chest, and the other one gets an IV started.

Rage like I've never felt scorches over every part of me. Wheeling around, I barrel toward Brent, whose eyes widen, and I pummel him with blow after blow to his face. "You sorry piece of shit!"

It takes both Chase and Jace to get me off of him. He lies bloodied and bruised, unconscious on the ground.

"I've got a faint pulse," a paramedic says.

"We need to stabilize her before we can move her," the other one barks.

"I think we should move her now, or we're going to lose her." The other paramedic is crushing a bag of fluid to get it into her body.

I help load her on a gurney and hold her cold hand. The paramedic tells Chase where they are taking her and tells them we'll be right behind them.

I watch them wheel her into the ambulance and walk back into the yurt, picking up the blanket her mother made her from the floor. "This is what he took from her house. The one thing that meant the most to her." I clutch it to my chest.

"I found Brent's keys. Take his car and head to the hospital." Chase throws them at me. "I'm going to make sure this asshole doesn't die, and then I'm locking him up." He nudges Brent's shoe with the toe of his boot.

"If you would have just let me kill him, you could be calling the coroner instead." I spit on the ground next to him and stomp to his car.

Jace loads into the passenger side. "I'm coming with you."

Dust fills the night air as I race down the mountain, still feeling rage surging through me.

"She's going to be okay. I know it," Jace tries to calm me. "We found her in time."

I remain silent as my head spins out of control, switching my thoughts back and forth between Thayer and Rachel. At this point, my mind can't tell them apart. Rachel lies on the forest floor, begging me to save her, while Thayer hangs from the end of a rope, gasping to breathe. I can't save either one of them. I'm wrecked with agony, and I run off the road, slamming on the brakes mere inches from crashing into a tree.

I'm in a fog, and my voice doesn't work. I can hear, but I can't move. Jace's door opens, and then mine with his hands on me. "Don't do this. I can't lose you too," he cries. "I know that look. I saw it years ago with Rachel. Thayer is not Rachel. She doesn't want to die, Blaise." He twists my face to his. "Do you hear me?"

I slowly nod.

"Move over and let me drive."

Sliding across the seat, I lay my head against the window, and it seems like everything from that point on moves in slow motion. I can hear Jace talking to me, but I can't take in what he's saying.

We go from darkness to streetlights flashing by the windows until the car comes to a standstill outside of a hospital. He opens his door and jogs to my side, and approaches me like an injured animal.

"Let me help you," he says, reaching across me and unfastening my seat belt.

He gets me on my own two feet, and I still. "I can't go in there."

"You can and you will because Thayer needs you," he says with sternness.

He doesn't let me back down, leading me into the emergency room, where Sage is pacing the floor. When she sees me, she runs into my arms.

"Thank God you found her, but they won't tell me anything."

My mind is numb, and I just stare at her.

Jace peels her off me. "Give him a minute," he tells her. "I'll see what I can find out."

I remain in the same spot, and he walks with Sage to the check-in counter. I see him take out his phone. He makes a call and hands it to the lady behind the counter. She listens, then gives it back to him, and the double doors swing open. Jace moves to my side. "I called Chase, and they are letting us in to the surgical waiting room."

I mindlessly follow him through the doors to the elevator, and we're greeted in the waiting room by a surgical nurse.

"Thayer is in surgery, and I wish I had more news for you other than it's touch and go. She's lost a lot of blood, and the bullet is lodged near her spine. We won't know if there are any permanent injuries until she wakes up."

"If she wakes up," I rasp.

The nurse casts her gaze to her feet.

"She's going to wake up. She's strong and a fighter," Sage snarls.

"I'll keep you updated." The nurse disappears through a set of automatic doors.

"What the hell happened?" Sage hollers.

Jace drags her to a chair, and they sit. I walk over to the window and look out over the town, feeling completely lost and empty. Not wanting to be here. Not wanting to be anywhere.

An hour passes, and I'm still staring out the window when a heavy hand lies on my shoulder.

"Hey," Chase says. "Are you alright? Jace says you haven't moved an inch despite him calling your name."

I swallow the dryness in my mouth. "No. I'm not okay, and I'm not sure I ever will be again."

"Blaise Calhoun," someone speaking my name has me turning around to see a man in scrubs.

"That's me," I say, walking toward him.

"I'm the physician who operated on Thayer Hawkins, and I have permission from her father to speak with you."

"How is she?"

"She's a lucky young woman to have survived the surgery. I removed the bullet, and from what I can tell, there was no permanent damage to the spinal cord. She'll have some acute swelling that may limit her, but in my professional opinion, she'll fully recover in time. Her father is getting on a plane and will be here by morning."

"Thank you." I shake his hand, holding back the tears that have been threatening to fall.

"Thank goodness she's going to be okay," Sage cries.

"We'll be taking her to the ICU, but I'm asking that you all go home. She won't be awake until morning, and we're going to keep a close eye on her," the doctor says and then leaves the room.

Chase ambles over to me. "I think we all could use some rest. I'll drive all of us home, and we can come back first thing in the morning."

"I'm not going anywhere," Sage says, planting herself on the wooden cushioned sofa.

Jace convinces her to come home with us, and we pile into Chase's truck.

"At least tell me the bastard is dead," Sage grumbles from the back seat.

"He's locked up and being attended to by a physician."

"Blaise beat the shit out of him," Jace tells her.

"Good, but I'd rather he be dead." She snaps her seat belt.

I don't recall the drive home, only being escorted into the house and then bombarded with questions from my family. Chase fills in the blanks as I storm up the stairs to my room and slam the door.

26

THAYER

"Dad." I blink, trying to open my eyes and clear the fuzziness from my brain. "Where am I?" I try to sit, and an alarm goes off.

"You're in the ICU. You were shot in the back by that no-good bastard."

"Is he...dead?" I begin to tremble.

"He's where he can't hurt you anymore." Chase appears behind my father, who is sitting on the edge of my bed.

I glance around him. "Where's Blaise? Is he okay?" I shake uncontrollably, and my dad eases me to the pillow.

"You've got to calm down. You're safe."

All sorts of awful things race through my mind. "Did he kill Blaise?"

"No." Chase's response is quick.

Everything rushes back in a flash. "Brent killed the man in the tent that was trying to help me." Overwhelming guilt fills my mind.

"No, he didn't. He tried but failed. He's in the hospital, and the doctors say he's going to be alright. He lost his spleen and a lot of blood, but we got to him in time, and you, thanks to the message you left on the mirror."

"The doctor stressed that you need to stay calm and relax." My dad rubs my arm in an attempt to soothe me.

"If Blaise isn't hurt, then where is he?"

Chase's gaze falls to his feet.

"Don't worry about him right now. You have to concentrate on getting better."

A doctor walks in with a nurse. "You're awake," he says, walking to my bedside. The nurse shuts off an alarm.

"You must be her father I spoke with on the phone two days ago."

"Yes." My dad stands, extending his hand and thanking him for saving my life.

"How long have I been here?"

"You've been sedated for two days to give your body rest. I'd like to test your reflexes," the doc states and draws back my sheets, and instructs me on what he wants done. "I'd say you're one lucky lady. That bullet was mere centimeters from your spine."

"He shot me in the back." I glance over my shoulder and then suddenly feel the tug of my skin. It wasn't a question, merely a memory.

"A little more to the right, and you would've been paralyzed from the neck down."

"When can I get out of here?" I start to sit.

"Not so fast, young lady." The doctor chuckles. "You'll need to be on IV antibiotics and have your labs monitored. You lost a lot of blood."

"I can't stay here. I have to find Blaise."

"Blaise will have to come to you." The doctor pats me on the shoulder. "Rest, and as soon as I feel you're ready, I'll send you packing."

"Daddy," I plead.

"I'll go find him." Chase storms out the door.

"I almost lost you." My dad's lip quivers, showing a kink in his steadfast armor of strength. He gently hugs me.

"I'm good," I assure him. "I'm only glad the nightmare is finally over."

"You're coming home where you belong."

"I have a life here that I love, and you don't have to worry about me anymore."

The door flies open, and Sage bolts into my arms. "You had me so scared," she openly cries, and I wince in pain at her hugging me. "Oh, I'm sorry." She lets go.

"It's okay." I wipe her tears with my fingers.

"I wanted to kill the bastard myself." Her tears turn to anger. "The beating Blaise gave him wasn't enough as far as I'm concerned."

"Blaise got to him?"

"Yes." She peers around the room. "Hasn't he been here?"

"He left yesterday at noon, and I haven't seen him since," my father tells her.

"He should be here," Sage scowls.

"After the things he's been through, he's probably scared and retreating to himself. That's why I have to find him and tell him everything is going to be alright."

Dad stands, crossing his thick arms. "If the man truly loved you, he'd be here."

"I'm sure he's hurting. You don't understand, he's—"

"I don't give a crap whether he's hurting or not. You're my priority. I get that he and his family saved you, but where the hell is he now?"

Sage speaks up. "I agree with Thayer. If he's not here, there's a reason. I've seen the two of them together, and he adores your daughter. I misjudged him once. I won't do it again."

I reach for her hand. "Thank you for sticking up for him."

"I know how happy he makes you and vice versa."

"That's yet to be seen by me, and I'm not leaving town until I know you're alright mentally and physically. He seemed pretty despondent to me yesterday. He barely spoke a word to anyone and stayed by himself in the corner of the room," my dad tells me.

My heart drums wildly. "He's withdrawing," I whisper. I can only imagine with his past what he must be thinking. I rush to get out of bed again, only to be stopped by the room spinning.

Sage steadies me. "I'll go find him for you."

"Chase went to look for him." Dad looks grim.

"Get back in bed, and I'll call Chase."

"Where's my phone? I'll call Blaise."

"I have your purse in my car, but use my phone." Sage takes it out of her bag. She unlocks it, handing it to me.

I find his number, and it rings once and then goes directly to voicemail. "Blaise, where are you? I need you. Please call me." I hang up.

"How about I get you something to eat?" my father offers.

"I could use a glass of water. My throat is parched."

"I'll run to the cafeteria and get a bottle of water and a bowl of soup. You're going to need to eat in order to get your strength back."

"Listen to your father," Sage says and ushers him out of the room. "I'm sure Blaise will show up any minute."

"I hope you're right, but I have a bad feeling about it."

She sits on the edge of my bed. "Do you recall what happened?"

"Most of it. Some of it's a little fuzzy. Brent was at the gallery. He saw Blaise and I come out of the dark room."

"How did he lure you to get into his car?"

"He said if I created a scene, he'd start shooting people. I couldn't have that on my conscious."

"Where was he taking you?"

"I don't know what his final destination was for me."

"Good thing he told you where you were going for the night, and you were able to tell someone."

"I was scared. He said if I didn't do what he wanted, he'd kill me and then hunt down Blaise."

"Bastard," she thunders.

At that moment, Blaise walks into my room with his gaze downward.

"Blaise." I breathe his name in a sigh of relief.

Chase moves around him. "I found him sitting in his truck in the parking lot. Why don't we give the two of them a minute?" He braces his hand on Sage's shoulder.

"You might want to entertain my father in the cafeteria for a bit," I say as they leave my room.

Blaise shuts the door behind them.

"Come here." I pat the mattress.

He keeps his gaze glued to the floor but inches toward me. "Are you okay?"

"You're the one in the hospital bed, and you're asking me if I'm alright?" His voice is void of any emotion.

I reach for his hand, and he takes a step out of my reach. "Don't."

"I know you're afraid with everything that's gone on in your past, but I'm going to be okay. The two of us will be safe. Brent is behind bars where he belongs, and the doctor said that I'm going to make a full recovery."

"I can't do this."

I ease to the side of the bed. "You can't do what?"

"Love you." He finally looks at me. "I can't love anyone."

"Don't shut your heart down, Blaise. You love me, and I know it. I've felt it in every ounce of my body." My chin trembles, and my eyes dampen.

"I feel nothing," he says coldly.

"That's not true. I know you. You feel too much."

"Not anymore." He swallows hard. "When I saw you bloody and laying on the ground lifeless, I relived Rachel's death all over again, but it was your face I was seeing, not hers. I won't allow myself to ever be put in a situation to lose someone I love ever again. I'm sorry. I just can't do it."

Steadying myself when I get to my feet, I stand as close to him as he'll allow me. "I'm not going anywhere, Blaise, and I get what your feeling, but there will never be another man for me but you. So, while you are healing, I'll protect my heart for you, and I'll wait for you to come back to me." My hand shakes as I touch his jawline, and he clenches his teeth.

"You need to move on and find someone else. I'm not the man for you. I never was. I'm sorry. I didn't mean to hurt you."

"You didn't hurt me, Blaise. You set me free to love again and be loved, which you did thoroughly, and you saved me from a madman."

"I'll never be free." He turns to walk away.

"I hope that's not true."

He wheels back around and kisses me deeply, so much so that I can taste his pain. "Goodbye, Thayer," he sniffs and marches out.

I ease back against the bed, crying, knowing how much pain he's in and the thought of losing him forever.

* * *

Two weeks later...

"Are you sure you don't want to hop on a plane and come back to the city with me?" My dad stands outside the airport, gripping his suitcase.

"I'm sure, Dad. Thank you for taking such good care of me." I hug him.

"If you change your mind, I'm a phone call away." He kisses the top of my head.

"Goodbye, Mr. Hawkins. I'll keep an eye on her for you." Sage joins us in our hug.

"I do feel better knowing your stalker isn't able to get out on bail, and it sounds like he'll be spending the rest of his life in prison."

"Chase will see to it that he's tried to the fullest extent of the law."

"He's a good a man. He and I will be in touch."

"You're going to miss your flight."

"I'll call you when I land." He waves as he walks away.

"I love your dad." Sage hooks her arm in mine.

"Me too."

"How are you feeling? Are you up to going to the brewery? I'm dying for one of their burgers."

"Sounds good."

"On second thought. Perhaps we should go somewhere else." She bites the corner of her mouth.

"I'm not going to steer clear of going to the brewery because I might run into Blaise."

"Suit yourself," she snorts and drives into town. "I'm honestly sorry about the way things turned out with Blaise."

"It's not over between us. He just doesn't know it yet." I shut the door, and we walk into the brewery arm in arm. We find a booth near the front, and we order margaritas and two cheeseburgers.

"I'm glad to see you've gotten your appetite back." She laughs.

"I'm feeling pretty good. Still a little sore, but considering being shot two weeks ago, I can't complain."

"You almost died. You still need to take it easy."

"Yes, Dad," I snicker.

My gaze is diverted when I see Blaise walk into the restaurant by himself and immediately sit at the bar. A waitress scurries up to him and starts flipping her hair over her shoulder and grinning, all while touching him any chance she can get.

I study him. There's a smile on his lips but not around his eyes. It's like they are dim, without emotion. Kind of like the first time I met him. He's good at pretending to be okay, but his body language speaks volumes. As if he knows he's being watched, he slowly turns his head and sees me. His gaze locks with mine for a long moment before he touches her arm and whispers something in her ear. Her head falls back in laughter, and she drapes her arms around his neck. Instead of hugging her, he puts his hands on her shoulders and moves her back.

"We can leave," Sage snarls.

"No." I take a sip of my drink and continue to watch him. He doesn't want her, it's obvious to me, but she's oblivious. He's looking at her, but he doesn't see her. I can tell he's going through the motions, and he wants me to be angry at him so that I'll forget about him. When I don't back down, his jaw tenses, but he doesn't touch her. She cluelessly leans down and pecks him on the cheek. Sage bolts to her feet, and I snag her hand. "Please don't. He's purposely trying to make me jealous."

"And I need to give him a piece of my mind," she growls.

"Sit," I tell her, and she reluctantly does.

"I can't believe he's doing this to you."

"That's just it. He's doing it to himself. He thinks he's protecting his heart, but I know what he felt for me is real, and he'll come to terms with it."

"In the meantime, he's hurting you."

"I'm not going to let it get to me." I toast my glass with hers.

"I hope he comes to his senses real soon, or else someone else is going to sweep you off of your feet."

"That's not going to happen. Blaise will be worth the wait. I'm sure of it."

27

BLAISE

T hree months later...

"Are you going to the grand opening of the gallery tonight?" Evie inquires, rocking her pen back and forth between her fingers.

"I don't think that's a good idea." I rest my arm on the back of the couch.

She lays her pen and pad of paper down and leans forward, placing her elbows on her knees, and stares at me. "Isn't it time you get your life back?"

"I don't know what that looks like without Thayer in it." I chew on my thumbnail.

"You've been living these last several months as a walking zombie. We've discussed at length what happened to Thayer in comparison to Rachel. What I don't understand, as an intelligent man, why you can't see the difference. Rachel made a choice to take her own life. Thayer fought to save hers. Instead of being happy she's alive and well, you buried her in your mind and heart as if she actually died."

I drop my hand and switch to gnawing on the inside of my cheek.

"Have you been with anyone since the incident?"

I shake my head. "I've lost all interest."

"Do you love Thayer?"

"Does it matter?" I look her squarely in the eye.

"Yes, as a matter of fact, it does." She gets up, and for the first time in all the sessions we've had, she sits beside me on the leather couch. "It's time for some tough love. You can either stay status quo with your emotions and grow old alone or choose to find a way to let go and have the life I know deep down you really want. The time you spent with Thayer, you were a different man. Happy and full of life, wearing an honest-to-goodness smile, not the fake one you plaster on to make everyone think you're doing okay. I know better."

"It's worked so far," I mutter.

"Then why do I get concerned calls from your cousins? Mercy and Jace, to be exact."

"Because neither one of them can leave well enough alone. Mercy shouldn't bother you anymore. She has her hands full with her new baby." I light up at the thought.

"Ah." She points to me. "That! Whatever you were just thinking brought about a true smile. That's the man everyone misses."

"Babies make everyone happy."

"Come on, Blaise. I know you want to be happy. Are you still having nightmares? Is that what's holding you back?"

"They've eased up a bit since you gave me something to help me sleep."

"Tell me something. When you look five years down the road, what do you see?"

"Nothing."

"Okay, let me reword my question. When you were with Thayer, what did you envision your life like five years from now?"

I exhale. "A wife, several kids, our own place."

"Was it full of happiness?"

I feel a grin tug at the corners of my mouth. "Pure bliss."

"You can still have that."

"She's probably moved on by now. Lord knows I've given her enough reasons to." I tap my index finger to my chin.

"How about you test out that theory at the gallery tonight. Find her, tell her how you feel."

I glance at my watch. "Our time is up. I'll see you in a week," I say, and her head droops downward. "Look, I know you want to fix me, but some things are just too broken." I walk out and go to Mercy and Hardin's like I promised her I would. She's been home for two days, and I haven't been by to see the new baby, and I don't want the wrath of Mercy at my feet.

"Hey," Hardin says, letting me in the door. "I'm glad you came. She's in the baby's room."

"Thanks." I walk through the house and see her sitting in the rocking chair, holding her son.

"It's about damn time you showed your face." She smirks.

My heart loses its heaviness the minute she hands him to me. "He's beautiful."

She rubs her lips together, and I know there's a lecture coming on. "I want my son to get to know the cousin I adore. Not the one standing in front of me, but the one who loves life. I think you've forgotten about him."

"Mercy, I..."

"Don't Mercy me. I'm done with your pitiful ass feeling sorry for yourself. You have a woman who loves you and is waiting for you to get your shit together."

"How do you know she is waiting for me?"

"She and I have had lunch several times, and I've had to talk her off a ledge not to move back to Boston because it breaks her heart to see you in town with other women trying to get your attention."

"They don't mean anything to me, and I thought it might help her get over me if she saw me out. I haven't touched one of them."

"It hasn't, and you're an idiot." She pops me on the back of the head. "Do you know how many people in this world would die to be loved like she loves you? Rachel did a number on you, but Thayer has done nothing but love you, and it's time you get your head out of your ass and make things right with her. Looking at you, holding my son, how can you say this isn't what you want for your life?"

"I do," I admit. "I want a wife and children, and Thayer is the only woman I'd ever give my heart to, but what if it's too late?"

"It's never too late to go after what you want. You need her as much as she needs you, and I'd say it's about damn time you go get her. You know where she'll be tonight."

I lick the tears from my lips. "I've been such a jerk."

"No, sweetie, you haven't. You needed time to heal." She hugs me.

"Do you really think she'll take me back?"

"There's only one way to find out."

I lift my wrist to check the time. "I better go if I'm going to make it in time."

"You've got a couple of hours." She laughs.

"I have an errand to run first and a phone call to make." I hand her Ethan. "He really is beautiful, just like his momma." I kiss her cheek. "Thanks for the kicking in the tail."

"Any time. You know I'm always good for one," she snorts, hollering at me rushing out the door.

While I get dressed, I make a call, not sure how it's going to go, but it doesn't matter because it's one of the most important phone calls I need to make. Once that is out of the way, I drive into town to one of the local stores and find exactly what I'm looking for. I kill some time with Walker in the bakery, and then we walk the block together to Kat's building.

There's a greeter at the door asking for our personal invitations.

"I...I don't have one." I pat the inside of my jacket.

"It's okay. He's with me," Walker tells him, and he lets us inside.

"I didn't know it was by invitation only."

"Sage didn't want the entire town flooding the place and kept the invitation to buyers and personal friends."

"I guess she took me off of that list." I chuckle.

As soon as we're inside the gallery, Sage storms in my direction. "You weren't invited." She crosses her arms over her chest. "I don't need you here flaunting your good looks in front of Thayer."

My gaze shifts to Thayer walking up beside her. "It's alright, Sage. He won't bother me."

Sage narrows her eyes. "I swear if you cause a scene, I'm going to have you removed."

I nod. "It's going to be a tough crowd," I mutter. "How have you been?" I direct my question to Thayer.

"What's that southern saying? Fair to middling?" Her lip curls into a smile, and my heart melts.

"You look beautiful. Lavender is definitely your color. Even better than pink." I sweep my fingertips down her arm.

She stiffens and jerks my hand to follow her, and we walk to the back of the gallery. She opens the door to the dark room, switching on the light. "You have some nerve. You haven't so much as looked my way in months, and you come here throwing on the charm and expect me to do what?" Her hands fly to her hips.

"I came here to tell you that I'm sorry for the way I've behaved. It's taken me this long to get my act together. I've never once stopped loving you."

She tosses her hands in the air. "That's so good to know," she says sarcastically. "Because I've watched women try to cling to you, and you give them nothing in return, yet you've washed your hands of me and don't even speak to me, but I'm supposed to believe you still love me?"

"I haven't slept with any of them."

"It doesn't matter if you did or not! You've had nothing to do with me!" Her volume rises.

"It matters to me. The only woman I want is you."

Tears fill her eyes. "I've waited to hear those words from you for what seems like forever, and now..." She looks away.

"Now what?" I touch her hand.

"I don't know. You broke my heart."

"I want to mend it back together."

"Until the next time something happens you can't handle?"

"I don't blame you for feeling that way, but no. I want forever." I get down on one knee and take a black velvet box out of my pocket.

"Don't." She shakes her head, and her tears fall.

"I love you, Thayer Hawkins, even though that's not the side you've seen of me the last several months, but there is no woman that owns my heart but you. I can't begin to tell you how sorry I am for pushing you away. My pain was so deep because I couldn't bear the idea of losing you. It tormented me when I saw you that night laying in a puddle of your own blood."

"Don't," she repeats with her eyes closed, shedding a stream of tears.

"I will tell you every day for the rest of my life how much I love you and need you. You saved me long before I rescued you that night. I hid myself from everyone but you. You saw me and loved me for the person you knew me to be on the inside, not the man I displayed to everyone else. I want to have babies with you and grow old together, holding hands and supporting one another."

"I couldn't marry a man without my father's blessings, and you'll never get it."

"I already have." I take out my phone and call her father, and put him on a video call.

"Hey, sweetheart."

"Daddy," she weeps.

"I know I've been extremely hard on Blaise these last few months, but I believed him when he told me how much he loves you. I'm pretty good at knowing when a man is honest, and my gut tells me he's telling the truth."

She looks at me and then back at him. "Really? You gave him your blessing?"

"If it's what you truly want and you love him, then yes."

"Thank you, Mr. Hawkins," I say and disconnect. "Do you?" I ask.

"Do I what?"

"Love me, or have I killed your love for me?"

"I wanted to hate you every day for the last three months." She presses her lips together.

"But..." I wait for her response.

"I don't hate you."

I open the box and hold out the ring. "Will you do me the honor of being my wife and spending the rest of your life with me?"

"No more running?"

I shake my head.

"No more fake smiles. You'll talk to me when things grow dark in that head of yours?"

"I promise."

"And you'll let me sleep with my mother's blanket." A smile creeps on her pretty face.

"As long as it doesn't come between us." My heart does a somersault waiting for her answer.

"You'll keep your wild side just for me?"

"Nobody else."

"No expiration date on our relationship?" She cocks a brow, knowing me so well.

"Is eternity long enough?"

She stares at me.

"You're killing me down here." I chuckle and take the ring out of the box. "Will you marry me, Thayer Hawkins?"

She presses her perfect lips together. "You've made me wait this long, and I need some time to think. The shindig is over in an hour. If you haven't changed your mind in that time frame, meet me back here, and I'll give you an answer."

I rise from the floor and sigh. "I'll see you in sixty minutes."

I follow her out, and I see Sage smirk at her like she thinks Thayer kicked me to the curb.

It's the longest sixty minutes of my life, pacing outside the building. When everyone starts to leave, I step inside, watching Sage start to lock up. Thayer walks over to her and whispers something in her ear. She hands her the keys and says, "I hope like hell you know what you're doing," then she shoots me a threatening glare.

Thayer waves me into the dark room, and I move quickly to follow her. "I have an answer to your question, but you have to ask me again."

I dig the ring out of my pocket and drop to one knee. "Will you marry me?" I hold my breath.

She extends her hand, and I slip the diamond on it. "Yes, Blaise Calhoun, I'll marry you."

I get to my feet and crash my lips to hers. "I've missed your taste so damn much."

"I've missed you too." She has both her hands on either side of my face. "I never stopped loving you."

"I'm so thankful," I say against her lips.

She bursts out laughing. "What is it about this dark room?"

"It's not the room. It's all you, baby, and I love you."

28

THAYER

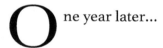ne year later...

"I can't wait to develop these photos of you in your wedding dress." Sage moves around me, snapping pictures.

"I wish you would've let me hire someone else to snap pictures so that you could relax and enjoy this day with me."

She stops shooting and peeks from behind the lens. "No way in hell would I trust this to anyone else. Besides, I'm most relaxed when I'm behind my camera." She resumes her clicking.

I stand in front of the full-length mirror in the small room at the back of the church. My father insisted his daughter get married in a church building in a traditional manner rather than a barn. I thought Blaise would be upset when I mentioned it because his cousins had been married on their property, but he was all on board. He said he'd marry me anywhere. A warm smile covers my face recalling the moment.

We found a church built back in 1866 by one of the original founders of Missoula when it was still part of the Washington territory. I fell in love with the old run-down church, and I didn't think we'd be able to use it because it required too many repairs. Blaise contacted the land owner and offered to pay for the renovations if he'd let us use the place since he had no interest in selling it. It had been in his family since it originated, and he wasn't about to let it go. He agreed to the renovations, and here we are, getting married today.

"You couldn't have picked a more perfect dress for you. Was your dad upset you didn't go with customary white?" Sage brushes the back of my lavender dress down with her hand.

"He squawked about it until I reminded him that it's my wedding."

"I personally can't wait until Blaise gets a load of you in this dress."

"It's his favorite color." My cheeks turn pink every time I think about the opening night of the gallery and his reaction to my lavender dress. I wear it on special occasions, and he always end up burying himself inside me in whatever space he can find the quickest. The brewery has banned us from going near their storage room.

"I want to make sure to get some good pics of you and your father before you enter the church." She hands me my white boutique of canna lilies. "They were my mother's favorite. She carried them on her wedding day," I say in a hushed voice. "I wish she were here."

"Oh, sweetie, I know you do, and I'm going to feel the same way on my big day about my mother." She brushes a stray tear from the corner of my eye. "None of that. You'll ruin your mascara."

"I have a surprise for Blaise."

"What is it?" She raises a quizzical brow.

I lift my lavender dress to my thigh and show her a red plaid garter belt I had to special order.

"Oh, my god, he's going to love it!" She snaps a picture.

"Make sure you're not shooting pictures of my...pink canoe." I laugh, thinking how much I adore Knox's dirty mouth. It's made for some funny banter in my books.

"I'll save those for the groom," she snorts.

I inhale, gazing at my reflection. "This is it. The day I've been waiting for."

"And you look beautiful," Sage drapes one arm around my neck from behind.

The past year flurries through my mind, going back to the day Blaise bailed on me. My heart begins the wild fluttering, and a sense of panic creeps into my throat. "Should I be doing this?" My voice cracks.

"What are you talking about?" Sage stares at me in the mirror.

"What if in a year or two Blaise walks about because his demons break out again?" I start to pace. "I couldn't handle him running. What if we have a kid or two. How would I raise them all alone." My hands fly in the air as I rant.

Sage grabs me by the shoulders and looks me squarely in the eyes. "You know if I thought Blaise wasn't the man for you, I'd be the first one to load you in a car and drive off to lord knows where. You love him, and he worships the ground you walk on. I have no doubts about the two of you."

"I need some air." I push past her and run out into the long hallway and out a side door, running in my heels to a massive oak tree, and I lean against it with my hands, breathing in and out large gulps of air.

I hear footsteps in the fallen leaves, and I stand tall, blinking back tears before I turn around. When I do, Blaise is ambling toward me wearing a dark gray suit, and he stops in his tracks. "You are the most beautiful thing I've ever laid eyes on. I love the choice of color." His gaze skims my body as his tongue sweeps out, licking his lips.

"You aren't supposed to see the bride before the wedding." My words are broken.

"What are you doing out here?" He takes a step toward me, and I hold my hand out, still carrying the lilies.

"Don't come any closer. I can't think when you're near me."

"What's there to contemplate?" He shoves his hands in his pockets like he used to do when he had his hands-off rule.

"I'm scared." My lip trembles.

"About what?" He frowns.

"What if you decide in a year or so you can't deal with whatever's going on in our lives, and you disappear into your dark place? Or what if it's just the meds keeping you in line, and you decide to stop taking them? Perhaps you wake up one day and don't love me anymore?"

With my last question, he storms toward me and covers my mouth with his hand. "Stop. None of those things are going to happen." He removes his hand from my mouth and laces his fingers with mine.

"How do you know?" My tears spill out.

"As to your first question, I've dealt with my demons. The second one, Dr. Shields took me off my meds six months ago, and I've been just fine. The third question is absurd. I will never not be madly in love with you, Thayer. It's not possible. You own me, heart and soul. I can't breathe without you."

"Are you sure? Like a hundred million percent sure?"

He laughs. "That's a big number, but I have no doubts. The day I asked you to marry me, do you remember the promises you wanted from me before you said yes?"

"Vaguely." I shake my head.

"Let me refresh your memory. You asked me about running. Have I done that?"

"No.

"Then you insisted on no more fake smiles and that I'd open up to you when things grew dark in my head. I haven't worn a fake smile since that day. Every grin on my face is genuine for you, and when I've felt the darkness come on, I ran into your arms."

I lift my chin and trail my fingertips on his jawline. "You have."

"And it was so easy to promise never to be with another woman because you're all I want and need." He kisses the tip of my nose. "The other thing you asked was about your mother's blanket. As tattered as that thing is, it's the best for cuddling with you because I know how loved and safe it makes you feel."

"Is that why every time we're buried underneath it, we end up making love?" My heart feels lighter being in his arms.

"That and the fact that I just like being balls-deep in you." He chuckles. "In fact, that's exactly where I'd like to be seeing you in this dress. Do you think the bark of this tree would scratch your back?" He looks at it, then presses his palm against it like he's seriously contemplating hiking up my wedding dress.

I playfully swat him in the chest. "Don't even think about it."

"Too late." He full on laughs. "But I left out the most important question you asked me."

"What was that?" I rasp, peering into his darkening eyes.

"You and I have no expiration date. I promised to love you until all eternity, and I'm a man of my word."

"You're still such the charmer." I kiss the dimple in his chin.

He wraps his arms around my waist and holds me close. "If I was that charming, I'd have convinced you to christen this tree with me." He dips his mouth to mine and sweetly laps his tongue with mine. "What do you say, city girl? Are you ready to marry the cowboy?"

I free myself from his hold and take his hand. "I don't want to wait one more minute."

* * *

Follow me on Amazon for all new releases.

Do you love military suspense? Check out the completed Revenge You Seek Series. Available on audible, ebook, and paperback.

PLAYLIST

Come Jesus Come by Stephen McWhirter

Hold On by Brandon Ray

Nobody Knows By Wayne Johnson

Want it Again by Thomas Rhett

My Person by Spencer Crandall

SERIES

Whiskey River West

Whiskey River Road

Elite Six Series

The Revenge You Seek

The Vigilante Hitman

August Series

Epic Love Stories

For more follow me on Amazon for a detailed list of books.

ABOUT THE AUTHOR

"This author has the magical ability to take an already strong and interesting plot and add so many unexpected twists and turns that it turns her books into a complete addiction for the reader." Dandelion Inspired Blog

Armed with books in the crook of my elbow, I can go anywhere. That's my philosophy! Better yet, I'll write the books that will take me on an adventure.

My heroes are a bit broken but will make you swoon. My heroines are their own kick-ass characters armed with humor and a plethora of sarcasm.

If I'm not tucked away in my writing den, with coffee firmly gripped in hand, you can find me with a book propped on my pillow, a pit bull lying across my legs, a Lab on the floor next to me, and two kittens running amuck.

My current adventure has me living in Idaho with my own gray-bearded hero, who's put up with my shenanigans for over thirty years, and he doesn't mind all my book boyfriends.

If you love romance, suspense, military men, lots of action and adventure infused with emotion, tear-worthy moments, and laugh-out-loud humor, dive into my books and let the world fall away at your feet.

CPSIA information can be obtained
at www.ICGtesting.com
Printed in the USA
BVHW050922230423
662871BV00028B/712